MISTY VALES HOWL... SECRET

A Werewolf Murder Mystery

Misty Vale Mysteries Book 1

ANDIE DANIELS

1

It was so early in the morning that it was only one step removed from night. The mist rolled in from the sea. Abbey walked with a purposeful stride towards the cliffs, surrounded by mist. Muttering distractedly to herself.

Reaching the cliff edge, she stumbled. Looking down, she saw the body of a male. His eyes stared lifeless. She shuddered, knowing he was dead, but she bent towards him anyway. Her fingers stretched to check for a pulse. Her hand shook as she reached to touch his neck.

Before touching the skin, the mist eased, and she saw his stomach was ripped open and raw flesh was visible, with blood congealed around the gash. With a gasp, she pulled her hand back, reversing away from the male in horror, trying to suppress the need to vomit. She closed her eyes, but the image was superimposed behind her closed eyelids. It was then she realised she had recognized the male. Jimmy Jones, owner of the bar in Misty Vale.

Misty Vale lay one step beyond the mist. The door only opened at dusk and dawn when the mist rolled in from the sea. It was a place for the Others to call home. Normals could not see the door, even when the mist was thick. Or rather, most normals could not see the door. But Abbey could.

She had returned to Ballybunion as an adult. Trying to recapture the happiness she had experienced there as a child when she had walked this beach with her great aunt. Her great-aunt explaining to her that you could tell the time from the sun. She had squinted at the sun, trying to read it like a clock, before her great aunt explained it was the position of the sun which told the time.

She had walked the beach, her mind wandering as dawn splashed across the cliffs, and she had walked into the mist and found herself in Misty Vale. Witches, vampires, werewolves, and all types of supernaturals were drawn there, and occasionally a normal.

When they stepped through the first time, a home awaited them. Abbey had stepped through that December dawn and found herself outside a bungalow on the edge of the town. Misty Vale was a haven for the Others. The werewolves could shift without fear. The vampires could walk in the sun. And the witches could perform their magic openly. The homes, each perfectly suited to its occupant.

Abbey straightened her spine. Taking a deep breath and suppressing a shudder, she approached the body. He was a large male, and Abbey was five foot seven, slim, although her figure had been described previously as boyish. This, unfortunately, did not mean she had a man's strength.

She examined the body, nodding to herself. She reached towards his neck and shoulders. She should be able to drag him into Misty Vale if she got her grip right. Preparing to shift him, she shook her head at her foolishness.

She stepped away and fished in her crossbody bag for her phone. She started taking photographs.

Stowing her phone, she looked at the body again. She approached, but this time at the foot of the body. She crouched down and grabbed the legs. Looking behind her, the door to Misty Vale was open. She pulled; he was a big male, and the going was slow, but she had no choice. She couldn't leave the body for the locals to find. An autopsy of the body would find more than the wound.

She stepped into Misty Vale, with only Jimmy's legs through the doorway. She was already sweating with the effort, and she shouted out for help.

A large male followed her through the Mist from Ballybunion. She had never seen him before. He stepped back out of Misty Vale, picked up Jimmy's body and carried him across the border.

Placing the body on the beach at Misty Vale. He turned his accusing blue eyes on her. "What did you do?" he said. He spoke with a deep timbre, but he had no distinctive accent.

"Do?" She gulped, her normally soft Irish accent sounding guttural in her shock. "I didn't do anything. I found him on the beach." She fished her phone from her bag and opened the photographs, passing him the phone.

He scrolled through the photographs. "Hmph," he said, using his fingers to zoom in on the body. His eyes opened wider, but he didn't say anything further, merely passed her back the phone.

"We should tell someone," she said.

"Who?" he asked, his eyebrows raised in question. "There is no law in Misty Vale," he told her.

"I know that," she said, flushing bright red. "But we can't just do nothing!"

"There is no law in Misty Vale," he repeated.

"Yes, but that is the problem," she said. "Why bother to dump the body outside of Misty Vale where it would cause trouble? When they could have left the body where they killed him, but instead, they dumped him outside?"

He nodded slowly, understanding that this was not about the murder. It was something else. Something that could endanger the haven. "I will get a car," he said, walking away with his back towards her. He called, "Stay with the body. I won't be long."

Abbey's legs shaking, she sunk to the ground. Misty Vale was home. The Others called it a haven, and it was a haven for Abbey, too. The outside world had left her battered and bruised. Her bruises from her last relationship had not only been emotional, but she had found the strength to walk away. She had returned to Ballybunion, hoping that it would help rebuild her soul, and she had found instead the magical haven of Misty Vale.

A shadow fell over her. She looked up; the man stood over her. Lost in her thoughts, she

8

hadn't noticed the time passing, and she hadn't heard him return. He reached his hand down to her, and she took it. His hand was cold as ice. Vampire, she thought, getting to her feet. They were always beautiful, and this one was no different, with his dark, nearly black hair, Roman nose, and square jaw.

She sighed; she was not afraid of vampires. They were no more dangerous than any of the Others. Murder was not against the law in Misty Vale. There was no law in Misty Vale, but crime was uncommon. And she had asked when she had first arrived, and no one had been killed in ten years or more.

"What's your name?" she asked.

"Sirius Winters," he said, raising his eyebrows in question, and she introduced herself. He nodded, turning to open the boot of a black sedan. He turned back around and picked up the body, placing him in the back. He closed the door. Nodding to her, he indicated to the passenger door and went around to the driver's side. She scrambled to the passenger door, afraid he would go without her if she didn't move quickly enough.

He drove away from the village centre, and Abbey suddenly realised what she had done. He had come along just as she had found the body. A body someone had dumped off the cliff at Ballybunion. Probably intending the sea to take it. She had been the only person to see the body. She had jumped into the car with a complete stranger, a vampire! No one even knew she had returned to

Misty Vale that day. If she disappeared, her friends would assume she had decided not to come back.

Sirius drove slowly, his eyes fixed on the road ahead, not paying her any attention. That was fine with her. The roads of Misty Vale were cement but rough and not conducive to driving at speed. This was rarely a problem. Misty Vale only made up a five-mile radius. So, speed was rarely necessary, and most residents didn't own a car. They were normally only used for transporting goods. Most places were easy to walk or cycle to. Abbey looked at Sirius. His hands held the steering wheel tightly, his knuckles were white, and his jaw was clenched.

She turned away, staring out the side window. Was she overreacting? Should she ask where they were going? He was larger than her. If he wanted to kill her, she didn't have a chance. The car began to slow, and Abbey looked around her.

They had pulled up to an old Tudor-style house with large oak trees on either side and potted plants in full bloom beside the door. The house was dark, and it looked like the occupants hadn't yet risen for the day. Sirius got out of the car and approached the house. Abbey thought, was this her chance to run?

He banged the knocker, and Abbey could hear the sound reverberating through the building. Abbey reached for the car door to get out. She saw the front door of the house open. A grey-haired woman with a surprisingly youthful face stood there.

Abbey sighed with relief. Climbing out of the car, he was bringing the body to someone else. The woman's hair was dishevelled, and she wore an old-fashioned flower-festooned dressing gown. Abbey approached the door.

"Well?" she said, looking at them both.

Sirius said nothing just went to the car, took the male from the back, and walked back to the house entrance. The lady stepped aside to allow him inside, and Abbey walked in behind him. He placed the body on the floor.

She looked at Sirius and then at the body. "If you are looking for a diagnosis," she said in a Boston accent, her eyebrows arched, "I can confirm he is dead."

Although Misty Vale was situated off the west coast of Ireland, its population was international. However, from what Abbey had seen, most residents were from Western Europe. She didn't know why this was.

"Yes," said Sirius, "we can see that. We want to know how he died and how long ago."

"Why?" she asked.

"I found him on the beach outside of Misty Vale," Abbey said, speaking for the first time.

Looking at Abbey, the older woman said, "Well, we best have some coffee," motioning for them to follow her. She led the way to the kitchen, leaving the body unattended. She directed them to the small bathroom off the kitchen where they could wash their hands.

Her kitchen was large and country-style. It had an old-fashioned stove as the centrepiece. She told them to sit down, and they took seats at the wooden table. She stoked the stove, adding timber to its belly.

She placed the coffee pot to brew, pulled scones from the fridge, and placed them on a tray and into the oven to heat. She then placed milk, sugar, butter, jam and coffee cups, plates, and cutlery on the table. Abbey felt awkward not offering to help, but the lady's self-sufficiency discouraged her from doing so. The coffee ready, the woman took the pot off the stove and placed it on a stand on the table. She fished the scones from the oven and brought them with her as she took a seat.

"I am Lily Andrews, Dr Lily Andrews. I know Sirius," she said. "But I don't believe we have met?"

Abbey had thought she was a doctor, but it was good to have it confirmed. "I'm Abbey, Abbey Williams."

"And you found the body?" she encouraged Abbey to tell the story.

"Yes, I was coming back to Misty Vale, having been in Dublin with my family for a few days. I was on the beach, waiting for the door to open. When the mist cleared, I saw him." She stuttered to a halt. "I realised I couldn't leave him on the beach for the normals to find. So, I took photographs and tried to drag him into Misty Vale. That's when I met Sirius. He carried him into Misty Vale for me."

"You have photographs? That could be useful." Abbey took her phone from her bag, opened the photograph app, and passed her the phone." Lily looked at the pictures and then handed it back to her. "Can you send me the photos?" she asked.

Abbey nodded, and Lily recited her phone number. Abbey sent them through right away. She put her phone back in her bag and selected a scone, adding butter and jam. She was surprised that she could eat after finding Jimmy like that, but the scones smelled delicious, and she suddenly felt hungry.

Lily sipped her coffee, a thoughtful look on her face. "It will take time for an autopsy. Two to three days minimum."

"Why so long?" Sirius asked.

"I will be able to do the physical exam quickly, but I will have to do a toxicology check, and that will need to be sent away. I don't have the facilities here. I will have to pull in favours to get it done."

"You will let us know when you have the results?" Abbey asked. Lily agreed to let them know. Abbey started to speculate about what occurred. But Lily warned it was better to wait for the results of the autopsy. She asked Abbey how long she had been in Misty Vale.

Abbey told her she had been living there for five months. They drank their coffee and ate their scones, speaking about the town and the diner. Abbey told them about Lydia, the diner owner, who had befriended her when she had first arrived. She told them how Lydia had helped Abbey with her confusion and fear of finding herself in this supernatural place. Abbey was surprised to see Sirius eating.

She had been here for five months, and she had never seen a vampire eat before. Sirius listened attentively to the conversation but rarely joined in. Once they had finished eating, Lily asked Sirius to carry Jimmy's body to the back room. Sirius picked up Jimmy and followed Lily. Abbey trailed behind him. Lily directed him to an examination room. She laid a plastic sheet on the examination bed, and Sirius put Jimmy down on top of it. She saw them to the door with promises to update them on her progress.

Outside, Sirius offered her a lift home, and Abbey took it with a deep sigh of gratitude. She gave him directions. Her fear and suspicion of Sirius had left her when they had arrived at Lily's house. Sitting in the passenger seat, she directed him to her home.

"You should let me have your phone number, and I will give you mine," he said. She took out her phone, and he recited his number for her to input it. She rang his number and hung up. Seeing they had arrived, she thanked him for the lift. She got out, happy to be home.

Abbey sat down on her couch; her mind was whirling. Jumping back up, she hurried to the kitchen. Digging in one of the drawers, she found a notebook. Hurrying to the hallway, she picked up the pen she had left there the other day. Heading back to the couch, she plopped down. Moving the pen to her right hand. "Body on the beach," she wrote.

Why dump the body?

Who would want to kill Jimmy?

What did Jimmy know or do that got him killed?

That made her stop and think. If Jimmy found out something that got him killed, then she needed to be careful. If she asked the wrong people questions, then she could be in danger.

At present, only four people knew Jimmy was dead: Lily, Sirius, her, and the killer. She needed to be careful while she was trying to find out who killed him. It was then she acknowledged to herself that she was going to solve the murder. She put the notebook and pen on the coffee table, pulling her feet up on the couch. She was asleep the second she closed her eyes.

Abbey woke a couple of hours later. The sun was shining in her front window. She yawned, rubbing her eyes. She brushed her fingers through her messy hair. Getting up from the couch, she went to the bathroom. She washed her hands and face and brushed her long, dark hair.

Checking herself in the mirror, her clothes looked fine, even though she had slept in them. She went back to the living room and collected her bag and notebook. She locked her door and headed back to the village. She had questions to ask, and she wanted to start with a friend.

Abbey walked into the diner. She saw Lydia, her friend and employer, behind the counter, serving a customer. Rick handed her a coffee without asking her for her order. Having worked together for five months, they all knew each other's orders. She thanked him. There was no charge for employees, but she left a tip.

"Could I pick your brain when you get a minute?" she asked Lydia.

Lydia said, "Of course," and Abbey took a seat at the back of the diner. There were already a couple of other customers waiting to be served. Abbey sipped her coffee and waited for Lydia to join her.

Abbey thought back to the first time she had found herself in Misty Vale. She had stood outside a bungalow. Looking around her, she didn't know where she was or how she had gotten there. She had been shaking her head and muttering like a mad person when she had seen a woman walking towards her.

Lydia had introduced herself, and she asked Abbey if she knew where she was. Abbey had said Ballybunion. Lydia had taken her arm gently, and Abbey had felt so confused she had been grateful.

16

"Why don't we walk back to the beach, and together, we will find your way home?" Lydia had said. Abbey had smiled, and she remembered how comforting those words had been.

Abbey had walked with Lydia, guiding her back to the beach. She saw houses she didn't remember from Ballybunion, and then they arrived at the village. Abbey looked all around at the village stores and the bar.

"Where am I?" she had asked.

"Misty Vale," Lydia had replied.

"So, we're not in Ballybunion anymore?" Abbey asked. Relaxing, she had only lost track of directions when she had been walking on the beach. She didn't remember a village called Misty Vale in the area, but she hadn't been there since she was a child.

"Yes, that's right, you're not in Ballybunion anymore." They were across from the diner. Lydia said, "Why don't we have a coffee before I show you the way back?"

Abbey had agreed. The diner had a glass front and glass door. Inside, there was a long counter with cakes and sandwiches behind a glass shield. There was a blackboard at the back with specials listed. Lydia had guided her to one of the small round tables that took up the space in front of the counter. Each table had four chairs with cushioned seats in a variety of colours. And individual menus sat on each table. The man behind the counter had come over, and they had ordered coffee.

Lydia had asked her to look around. Abbey hadn't understood why, but she had glanced around the diner. She then looked back at Lydia, her brow furrowed.

"Look again," Lydia told her. "Look closer. Look at the people."

Abbey had looked. They were normal people. Then, looking at them again, she realised they didn't look normal. They looked anything but normal.

Abbey pulled herself from her memories when Lydia sat down across from her.

"You look worried, what's the problem?" Lydia asked. Taking a mouthful of the coffee she had brought over with her.

"Jimmy Jones is dead," Abbey said.

Lydia looked shocked. "What happened?"

"I don't know. I found his body on the beach in Ballybunion this morning. It was not a natural death. I am hoping to find out what happened. What do you know about him?"

Lydia gasped. "Not much," she said. "He has lived here about ten years. He is the owner of McCafferty's Bar."

Abbey nodded; she had known he was the owner of the bar.

"He is a werewolf, but he is not part of the clan."

Abbey had suspected that Jimmy was a werewolf but hadn't been sure.

When she had looked around at the people that first day, she had noticed that many of them were not normal or average. If you saw the people

18

of Misty Vale individually, nothing marked them as different. But seeing them together, what you noticed most was that no one was average. Everyone stood out. Some were stunningly beautiful; some were excessively muscular, and some had piercingly vivid eyes that seemed to glow. All had something that drew attention.

Jimmy had been muscular, and she had always assumed he was a werewolf but had never had it confirmed.

Contrary to the stories that she had read prior to arriving in Misty Vale, werewolves did not run in packs. When she had met her first werewolf, she had asked her about her pack. Belinda had been horrified and had declared that she was not a dog. Belinda had informed her that she was a member of the local clan.

"Do you know anything else about Jimmy?" Abbey asked.

"Not much," Lydia replied. "I know he was aggressive but protective. He had put himself in the position to protect people weaker than himself. It has made him several foes over the years."

"Foes or enemies?"

"Foes, I think. I don't know of anyone who would have wanted to kill him. But as I said, I didn't know him very well. The staff at the bar probably know him best."

The queue at the diner counter was starting to build up, and Rick needed help. Lydia excused herself to get back to work.

Abbey knew her next stop would be the bar.

Chapter 3

Abbey walked down the street. McCafferty's bar had a dark red frontage and heavy wooden door. Abbey knocked; it was too early in the day for the bar to be open. She didn't know any of the staff. Her only hope was that someone was already there to get ready for opening later. There was no answer, so she knocked again, harder this time. She didn't want to have to speak to the staff when the bar was open.

"You will have to knock harder if you want anyone to hear you," came the masculine voice behind her. She stiffened, recognizing the voice at once as Sirius. She turned towards him. "What are you doing here?"

"The same as you, I expect," he said.

An arm reached over her shoulder, and Abbey felt an involuntary shiver down her spine. He knocked hard on the door. There was still no answer, and she was about to give up when the door crept open. A handsome black mountain of a man with a beard towered over her; he was even taller than Sirius. He looked to be in his early forties. He had a scowl on his face, and he barked, "We're not open," and tried to close the door on them.

Sirius raised his hand, stopping the door from closing. "We are not looking for a drink. We are here to talk about Jimmy," the other man growled and stepped back, letting them enter.

"Where is Jimmy?" the man asked.

21

"We haven't met before; my name is Sirius, and this is Abbey."

"Bill," the other man replied.

"He is dead," Sirius answered before Abbey could say anything. "His body was found this morning on the beach. We don't know what befell him."

Bill's face turned ashen. "Where is his body?" he asked.

"We brought him to the doctor and asked her to examine him to try to find the cause of death. There are signs that it may not be natural," Sirius told him.

The door to the kitchen, at the back of the bar, opened, and a young woman entered the bar. She had light blond hair and was very slim. She looked at Bill and walked to him without making eye contact with her or Sirius. "What are they doing here?" she whispered to Bill. But Abbey still heard her.

"Jimmy has been murdered," Bill told the young woman. Her knees seemed to go out from under her on hearing this. Bill wrapped an arm around her back to keep her from falling. He brought her over to a table, and Sirius took a chair down from the top of it for her to sit on.

"We don't know if it was murder," Abbey said, but she believed it was. She didn't want to be telling people Jimmy was murdered and then the autopsy finding out that it had been an accident. Also, if it was murder, she didn't want to tip off the murderer that they were asking questions. The more people who were connected with Jimmy they told, the more likely they were to come across the killer!

Bill snarled. "We want the body to bury when the doctor is finished, and we want the results of the exam." Abbey was sure he was a werewolf, not only by his build but his growling and snarling were faintly animalistic. She knew Belinda would be horrified at her racial profiling.

"Perhaps we could all sit down," she suggested. Without waiting for assent, Sirius took the remaining chairs off the table. Bill grunted but took a seat. She sat down, and Sirius followed.

"I'm Abbey, and this is Sirius," she said to the young woman.

"Sarah," the young woman introduced herself in a weak voice.

"Would you like tea? I can make it for you," she offered. The young woman shook her head.

"Do you think anyone would have wanted to hurt Jimmy?" Abbey asked, directing her question to Bill. She got to the point quickly, as she could see that Sarah was in shock and not likely to be able to answer questions.

"No, I can't think of anyone who would want to hurt him," Bill replied. She was surprised by this answer, given what Lydia had told her.

"You don't know of anyone he might have got on the wrong side of?" Abbey asked.

"No one that immediately comes to mind," he responded.

"Is there anything missing from the bar?" Sirius asked.

"Nothing that I've noticed," Bill said.

"Is there anything you can think of that might be relevant in trying to find out what occurred." This time, Abbey directed her question to Sarah.

"No," Sarah answered quietly.

Sirius arose, and so did Abbey. It was obvious that they were not going to get any answers here.

"I will see to it that the body is released to you, and I will send you the results," Sirius said, passing his phone to Bill for him to enter his contact details. "But let me make it clear there will be no further violence from this. If someone in Misty Vale is found to be responsible, I will ensure that they are dealt with. There is no law in Misty Vale, but I assure you that, in this instance, I will make myself the law."

Abbey believed him.

"That was interesting," she said, the bar door closing behind them.

"Indeed!"

Bill and Sarah were not talking. Abbey didn't know why. Maybe the clan knew something? She would have to talk to Belinda. She was the only clan wolf that she knew.

"I think the only thing to do now is to wait for the results of the autopsy," Sirius said.

Abbey nodded. "Okay."

"Can I drop you somewhere?" Sirius asked. Walking to his car.

"No, thank you. I have some errands to run," she said.

He said, "Goodbye," and headed to his car.

She looked at her watch. It was already late afternoon. She didn't know where the time had gone. Belinda's house was out on the far side of the village, near the woods. It would take her a good hour to walk to, and it would be full dark by then. The clan gathered there, and Abbey didn't know if they would welcome her. Especially if she was asking questions which people did not want to answer. She decided to ring Belinda instead. She selected Belinda's number on her phone. She answered after a couple of rings.

"Abbey," she said by way of greeting.

"Belinda, I wondered if you are around the village and if you are free to talk? I need some information?" Abbey said.

"Information?" Belinda queried.

"I would rather talk in person. It's sensitive," she replied.

"I won't be free until after eleven tonight. Why don't we have a drink in my house? I could collect you from your home at midnight, and I will drop you off afterwards?"

Abbey agreed and hung up.

She looked at the clock on the sitting room wall. Eleven Fifty, Belinda would be there soon to collect her. She had gone straight home after ending the call. The whole day had been draining, and she couldn't believe it was still the same day! She had only found Jimmy's body that morning!

She had made herself some dinner and had a shower. She washed her dark hair but didn't bother to style it. She just plaited it. She had changed into her lounge clothes, looking in the mirror. Her green eyes were all red and bloodshot. She was afraid if she didn't have a nap, she would fall asleep while talking to Belinda.

She gave up an hour later; she couldn't sleep, and after tossing and turning, she got up. She had dressed herself in jeans, a warm sweater, and her winter boots. The only thing to do was watch television until Belinda arrived a couple of hours later.

She saw the lights of Belinda's car pulling up outside, wondering if word of Jimmy's death had gotten out yet. She didn't wait for Belinda to knock; she picked up her bag, put on her coat, and went out to meet her.

She jumped into the car, and she saw Belinda's face. It was pale and serious, in stark contrast to her jet-black hair, which flowed around her face.

"You heard?" Abbey asked.

"Yes, you found his body?"

"Yes," Abbey confirmed.

"Okay, don't talk now. We will sit down and get you a drink," Belinda told her, pulling the car away from Abbey's house.

Abbey agreed gratefully. She didn't want to have this conversation in the car.

They arrived at Belinda's cabin. She had left a light on, and it felt welcoming. Abbey sat down, and Belinda brought her a glass of red wine and one for herself.

"How are you?" Belinda asked.

It was the first time someone had asked that. "I hardly know," Abbey said. "I haven't really thought about it. I can't believe it was only this morning. I didn't know Jimmy that well. Just served him in the diner."

Belinda nodded.

"He used to come in once a week for dinner. He was always very nice, left a good tip! Polite, that's all."

Abbey was surprised at how upset she was now that she was thinking about it. Belinda reached out and touched her hands. It was only then Abbey realised they were shaking. She took a mouthful of her wine, letting the rich flavour and the alcohol soothe her. "I need to find out who killed him," she told Belinda. "I know I won't be able to get it out of my mind if the killer isn't found."

"You're sure he was murdered?" Belinda asked.

"Yes, I'm sure. Dr Andrews is doing an autopsy, but I know it was murder. I saw his body. I saw him lying there on the beach, and I knew it was murder," Abbey said, taking another big gulp of her wine.

What can I do?" Belinda asked.

"I need to know everything you know about Jimmy. His relationships with the bar staff? Who he was friends with? Who he wasn't friends with?"

Belinda nodded.

"And I need to know about his relationship with the clan?"

Belinda started telling her everything she could think of. After a while, Belinda opened another bottle of wine. Abbey was feeling the effects of the wine when the day fully caught up with her. Belinda made her a cup of coffee before offering to drive her home.

Abbey walked carefully but steadily out to the car. Thankful that her friend, as a werewolf, didn't absorb alcohol the way normals did and was able to drive her home.

The drive through the village was sedate, even though it was deserted. She glanced at the bar; it would have closed a couple of hours ago. She spotted a dark figure coming from around the side of the bar. Must be one of the employees closing the bar, she thought. But the figure stepped forward, and the car light illuminated his face for a second. Sirius, what was he doing there? She nearly asked Belinda to stop so she could question him. She thought better of it. If he was up to no good better for him not to know she had seen him.

Besides, with the alcohol in her system, she was in no condition to deal with a vampire!

Chapter 4

Abbey woke the next morning at ten. Her head was a little sore, but she had an elixir that Lydia had made for her for just such an occasion. The first time she had used the elixir, she had remarked to Lydia that it worked like magic. Lydia had gently informed her that it was because it was magic. Abbey laughed. Of course it was magic. This was Misty Vale. She was glad she had it now. She had work today, but not until noon. She took the elixir that she kept in the bathroom cabinet and had her shower.

Sitting down with her coffee and toast, she remembered about Sirius coming out the side exit of the bar after it had closed. What had he been doing there! And what was his connection to Jimmy? And maybe she should be asking her friends about him. Yes, he had brought the body to Dr Andrews, but why did he care? What did it matter to him if the killer was found?

Sirius coming out of the bar after it was closed was suspicious. At the very least, he knew something he wasn't telling her. She needed to find out what he knew or what he was up to.

In the meantime, Belinda had given her another avenue to investigate. Belinda had told her that Jimmy had been in a fight with one of the clan wolves. A young cocky wolf called Jeff. She didn't know for sure, but she had heard it was about a woman. Jimmy had been in fights with clan wolves in the past. But she didn't think anyone was holding a grudge.

Wolves didn't hold on to resentment. They solved their issues with fights. Belinda had agreed to introduce Jeff to her at the bar tonight. She would have a chance to check him out. Belinda had also said that Kane, the leader of the clan, didn't get on well with Jimmy. But Belinda had reassured her that if Kane had wanted to kill Jimmy, he would have issued a challenge.

Abbey finished the last of her coffee. It was time to get on with her housework. Misty Vale may be a magical place, but some things were universal. Lydia had told her that the magic of Misty Vale supplied a home for anyone invited to the haven. She had told her that the bungalow was her home for as long as she chose to live in Misty Vale.

Abbey thought about how she had walked with Lydia to the village that first day and saw the people. Lydia had drawn her attention to how unusual they were. Abbey had shaken the impression off, and they had left the diner. Lydia had guided her to the beach in Misty Vale, and they had walked together through the mist. Abbey had found herself back on the beach in Ballybunion. She had looked around, trying to see her way back to Misty Vale, but it was hidden. She laughed to herself now at her disbelief and confusion.

Abbey finished the last of the housework and put on some laundry to wash before heading to work.

There was no time to talk to Lydia as a customer had arrived, and the midday rush was

30

only beginning. The diner was the only place in the village for lunch or coffee, so it was busy most of the time. It closed at six in the evening, and if you wanted to eat out after six, the bar was the only option.

The first break in customers came at about three forty, and Lydia had come over to ask Abbey how she was. Abbey knew she must look the way she felt. She hadn't slept well the night before, and when she had slept, she had woken from bad dreams that she only vaguely remembered. Abbey had only had time to reassure Lydia that she was okay before the rush started again.

Lydia had turned the sign on the door to closed at five-fifty, and Abbey had sighed with relief. They had started the clean-up.

"How are you?" Lydia asked.

"I'm okay. I didn't sleep very well last night, but I suppose that's not unexpected."

"Did you find out anything else about Jimmy?"

"I spoke to Belinda last night, and she told me of a young wolf that Jimmy had a run-in with. Belinda is going to introduce me to him later tonight. But what do you know about Sirius?"

"Sirius? The wizard?"

"Wizard?" said Abbey, her eyebrows raised in surprise.

"Yes, wizard. Did you not know he was a wizard?"

"No, I thought he was a vampire?"

"Why did you think he was a vampire?" Lydia asked.

"His hands were cold," Abbey said.

"Ah, so if someone has cold hands, you assume they are a vampire?"

"Well, no, I mean yes, but not only his hands. He looks like a vampire," she said.

Lydia raised her hands in question.

"He is beautiful," she said, "and he has those piercing eyes!"

"Okay," said Lydia. "He is handsome, and he does have piercing eyes, but he is not a vampire. He is a wizard. Older wizards often have very distinctive eyes," Lydia informed her.

"Older?" asked Abbey.

"I'm not sure how old, but definitely over two hundred years old."

Abbey gasped.

"He is one of the oldest residents of Misty Vale," Lydia told her. "I know he is the most powerful wizard in Misty Vale. It seems like he knows everyone, but he is very private. I have seen him with Tobias."

"Tobias?" Abbey asked.

"You don't know him?"

Abbey shook her head.

"He is an old vampire. You will recognise him as a vampire because his skin is very cold, he is exceptionally beautiful, and he has piercing eyes!"

"Ha, ha, very funny," Abbey said, throwing her eyes to heaven.

32

They finished the cleaning, and Abbey went to the back room to leave her apron in the laundry to be cleaned and picked up her coat.

She walked home slowly; it was a nice evening, and the sun had not yet set.

Chapter 5

Abbey walked into the bar, glancing at her phone. Belinda should be here by now. She spotted Belinda immediately and nodded hello before approaching the bar. The bartender was not Bill, and she could not see Sarah either. She paid for her drink and went over to join her friend.

"He's not here yet," Belinda said.

"Do you think he will come later?" Abbey asked.

"Yes, he comes every night," Belinda told her. "But I have some more information for you," she said. "I asked some of the clan wolves if they had noticed anything unusual about Jimmy in the run-up to his death. Everyone who had seen him said that he seemed either normal or a bit distracted. But there is something else." Belinda paused. "Karen, she is a clan wolf who is close to Sarah's age, and they are still good friends. She said that she had seen Sarah earlier that day, and she was blank," Belinda said.

"Blank?" Abbey asked.

"Yes, she said that Sarah walked right past her. She said that she had called out to her, and it was like she was in a trance."

"Now that is interesting. I wonder what was wrong with her?" Abbey asked.

Belinda shrugged.

"This was the morning before Jimmy was murdered. He was murdered sometime that night between when the bar closed at around midnight and when I found his body on the beach at dawn."

34

Abbey pinched at her lips with her fingers. She felt that Sarah's odd behaviour that morning was connected, but she didn't know how. She shook her head; she would have to think about it further, but not right now.

"Do you know if Sirius knew Jimmy?" she asked.

"Sirius? He was with you when you found his body?"

"Yes," Abbey confirmed.

"I don't know if he knew him well. They wouldn't have been friends. I don't think Sirius is friends with anyone. But then I only met him for the first time ten years ago. He had been away from Misty Vale for some time and only returned then," Belinda told her.

"Lydia said that Tobias would know Sirius best. Do you know Tobias?"

"I know of him, but I don't know him personally. He doesn't have much to do with the wolves."

"So, it's true that vampires and werewolves are enemies?" Abbey asked.

"How many times have I told you to stop believing in human fairy tales," Belinda said.

Abbey laughed; they had had this conversation many times.

"Why are you suddenly interested in Sirius? I thought he was helping?"

"I don't know, I just think he isn't being completely transparent with me. I think he knows more about Jimmy than he is saying," Abbey said.

"I'm afraid I can't help you there. I don't know much about Sirius or Tobias. But Jeff has just arrived."

Abbey took a sip of her drink. "Should we…?"

Belinda shook her head. "No, let's watch him for a while and let him have a drink and relax. We don't want to pounce on him the second he arrives and put him on alert."

Abbey nodded in agreement and relaxed back in her chair. She watched Jeff as inconspicuously as possible. He was bouncing with excitement. He didn't look like someone who had committed a murder yesterday. He was smiling and laughing with his friend, another young wolf by the looks of him. He kept looking around the bar and at the door to the back room like he was waiting for someone. She wondered if it was a woman. And if it was the woman that Belinda had heard Jeff and Jimmy arguing about?

Abbey and Belinda chatted and drank their drinks. Abbey wasn't particularly enjoying the drink; she had drunk too much at Belinda's house last night and had no appetite for more alcohol. She saw Bill come from the back room, wiping his hands with a cloth.

He went over to one of the beer taps and pulled it, draining the liquid from the glass into the sink, then nodded. He took an order from a customer and placed the money in the cash register. He served a couple of other customers and then frowned. He was frowning at Jeff.

That was interesting.

Did he know something about the argument? Did Bill suspect Jeff of being the murderer?

Sarah came out of the kitchen carrying a tray of food. She brought it over to a table at the front of the bar room. She smiled at the customer when she delivered the order. But her mouth turned down as soon as she turned away. Abbey could see the grief on her face. Bill came out from behind the bar to Sarah. He put an arm around her shoulders and turned her back towards the kitchen.

Jeff stepped in front of them before Sarah could reach the door. He stretched for Sarah, and Bill grasped his arm, stopping him from touching her. Bill's shoulders were tense, and he looked ready for a fight. He said something to Jeff, but Abbey couldn't hear what he said. She turned to Belinda.

Belinda shook her head. "I can't hear what they are saying. Even my wolf hearing can't hear over the noise of the bar. But I think we have found the woman that Jeff and Jimmy were fighting over," she said.

Abbey's eyebrows raised. "Sarah?"

Belinda nodded.

The noise in the bar died down, and the argument became the centre of everyone's attention.

"So, you are setting yourself as her hero, old man?" Jeff sneered at Bill.

Sirius placed himself between Bill and the male, seeming to have appeared out of nowhere.

"Do you know the terms under which the haven of Misty Vale applies?" he asked the young wolf. His face was a mask of anger, but his tone was soft. The male reared back at the menace coming from Sirius. He didn't answer, and Sirius continued, "Here, you are free to let your beast roam. But you are not free to take away the sanctuary of Misty Vale from others. I urge you to take care, or you may find your welcome here removed."

"This is not the only haven you know," the young wolf responded. His fear was not hidden by his hard voice.

"Oh," said Sirius, "you don't know? If you are unwelcome in one haven, you are unwelcome in all."

Abbey could see the shock on the faces of the others on hearing this. But the male's face was a rectus of horror at this news.

"That can't be true," he said.

"It is true," said the male who stood beside Sirius. Abbey didn't know who he was, but she suspected that this was the vampire, Tobias. The vampire was the acknowledged oldest resident of Misty Vale. He was very beautiful, his hair was white-blond, and he had piercing eyes such a dark shade of blue they were almost violet.

Jeff backed away from Sirius and Sarah. Sarah collapsed in relief, but Sirius placed his arm around her back to hold her up. He motioned with his other hand to Bill, who came to take her from him. He walked with Sarah to the kitchen and disappeared inside.

Jeff went back to where he had left his pint, downed it, and left without a backward glance at Sirius.

Abbey took a deep breath. She had been holding it unconsciously while the drama had unfolded.

Sirius had come to the bar. Had Abbey misunderstood what she had seen last night? Had Sirius been at the bar drinking and merely been the last customer to leave?

"I'm afraid meeting Jeff is off the cards for tonight," Belinda quipped.

Abbey turned her eyes away from Sirius, having momentarily forgotten Belinda.

Belinda raised her eyebrows.

"Yes, that seems to be the case," Abbey replied distractedly.

With the drama ended, the customers resumed their conversations, and the noise level went back to normal. Abbey noticed Sarah coming back out from the kitchen and starting to clean a table. Sirius approached her. He placed a hand on Sarah's shoulder and leaned close to her, speaking quietly into her ear. Abbey felt her breath catch in her chest, and she frowned. Sarah smiled gently at Sirius, the first smile Abbey had seen on her face. Sirius nodded and walked away, Abbey's eyes following him.

"That was interesting," said Belinda.

Abbey turned back to Belinda. "Yes, it was," she said.

"Well, this is your chance to meet Tobias?" Belinda suggested. Nodding towards where Sirius stood with the vampire. He was looking at Abbey.

Abbey stood and walked over to Sirius. "I didn't know you were such a regular at the bar?" she said.

"Regular?" he asked. "This is only my second time here in a long time. Although I was a regular here ten years ago," he said, a deep frown taking over his face. He then shook his head, removing some unpleasant thought. The first time I have been back since then was with yourself yesterday!"

Well, that answered Abbey's question. Sirius had not been the last customer at the bar last night. But had he been here for another reason? Was there something between him and Sarah? Had he been visiting Sarah last night? Abbey felt a sinking in her stomach at the thought. She didn't know why she felt uncomfortable at the idea that Sirius was involved with Sarah. It was probably the age difference. Sarah looked barely out of her teens, and Sirius was two hundred years old. But maybe at that age, any woman less than eighty should be considered too young!

Abbey covered her incorrect assumption that he had been drinking in the bar last night with a wry smile.

"Who is your friend?" she asked.

Sirius seemed nonplussed by the query but turned to the vampire and said, "Tobias, may I introduce Miss Abbey Williams." Tobias reached out a hand for her to shake. "Abbey, this is Tobias

Jacobson, the acknowledged oldest resident of Misty Vale."

Abbey shook the vampire's hand, mumbling, "Nice to meet you."

"Oldest?" Tobias said. "Or longest continuous resident?"

Sirius smiled, and Abbey felt that she was missing a private joke.

Abbey was unsure how to continue. She had wanted to meet Tobias to ask questions about Sirius, but she could hardly do that while Sirius stood beside them. However, she might not get another opportunity, so she asked, "How long have you known Sirius?" She felt Sirius stiffen beside her.

"Oh, it feels like forever," the vampire replied cryptically.

Out of the corner of her eye, Abbey saw Sirius relax. "So, you have been friends a long time?"

"What is a long time in the life of a normal can be merely a moment in the life of one such as I," Tobias replied.

Abbey knew she could not ask him anything detailed while Sirius listened, and it was obvious he was not going to be forthcoming with any information about him. Especially if he wouldn't even answer such a simple question. She would have to try the doctor. She had seemed to be comfortable around Sirius when they had dropped Jimmy's body at her house.

"You are a regular at the bar, I take it?" Sirius asked, re-joining the conversation. Abbey wasn't sure if he wanted the answer or just wanted to change the topic. Maybe he was self-conscious about his age. The vampire was probably the only Other here who was older than him.

"I wouldn't say I am a regular, but I have been here a few times," Abbey replied. Abbey decided to try a different track. "That was interesting," she said, "with Sarah and that young werewolf?"

"Indeed," Sirius replied.

"I didn't hear what he was saying?" Abbey asked.

"It appears that the wolf has a romantic interest in Sarah, which she does not reciprocate. Apparently, Jimmy was assisting Sarah in discouraging the boy," Sirius responded.

Boy! Abbey thought he was young, maybe twenty-seven, but hardly a boy. But if he thought that Jeff was a boy, then maybe he wasn't interested in Sarah and thought of her as a child, too?

"Do you think he would have…" She didn't need to finish the sentence.

"No, I don't think he would have gone that far."

If Sirius was involved in Jimmy's murder, then it didn't make sense for him to remove the suspicion from Jeff.

"Okay, I just wondered," Abbey said. She excused herself with a wave to Tobias and returned to Belinda.

"Any useful information?" Belinda asked when she returned to the table.

"Tobias is not going to be supplying any information about Sirius. He wouldn't even answer as to how long he had known him. Sirius did say that Jeff was interested in Sarah and that Jimmy was trying to discourage him. He also said that he doesn't believe that Jeff killed Jimmy. I don't think I can learn anything else tonight. But I think Dr Andrews knows Sirius well. I am going to visit her tomorrow to ask about the autopsy and Sirius."

Chapter 6

Abbey woke early; it was her turn to work the morning shift. It was going to be a long day, as she had agreed last week to cover Rick's shift today as well. She was going to be very tired when she finished that evening. She was sorry she had agreed to cover for him. It meant that she wouldn't get to speak to Dr Andrews until later that evening. She might even be in touch with the results of the autopsy herself before Abbey finished work.

Abbey wanted to know the results of the autopsy. She was at a dead-end as to where to go next with the investigation. Dead-end, that was the story of her life. She had always worked in jobs with no prospects.

But did she really think that she would be able to find Jimmy's killer? Who was she, an employee at a diner! Before she had found Misty Vale, she had worked in a dead-end office job. The closest she had to investigative knowledge was all the mystery books she had read. Even with the results of the autopsy, did she think she had the skill to understand them. But she wanted the excuse to visit Lily and ask about Sirius. And even though her investigation was probably useless, she was going to do the best she could to find the killer and make him pay. She found Jimmy's body; she would do everything she could to get justice for him.

Abbey had hurried to work. The day was never-ending. At the end of the day, she was glad when Lydia turned the sign to closed. Abbey started to clear the last table. "Leave that," said Lydia.

"What?" Abbey asked. Turning to her.

"Head off, you said you want to visit the doctor about the autopsy, and you have been looking at the clock all day! Head off now. I will finish the clean-up."

"Really?" Abbey asked.

"Yes, head off now," Lydia repeated.

"Thank you so much. I will do the full clean-up the next time," she promised. She dashed to the bar room, not waiting for Lydia to change her mind. Giving her friend and boss and quick hug, she hastened to the door.

She arrived at the doctor's house in thirty minutes but was somewhat breathless when she got there. She stopped outside and took a few deep breaths before knocking on the door. The doctor was surprised to see her. "I haven't received the result of the toxicology exam yet," she said by way of greeting.

"I am sorry for calling uninvited, but I was hoping to have a chat?"

The doctor's eyebrows raised. "Well, you best come inside," she said. She led Abbey back to the kitchen again. Abbey took a chair at the table. "What can I help you with?"

Abbey didn't think it was a good idea to jump right to ask about Sirius. So, she started by asking about the initial findings of the examination of Jimmy's body. Addressing her as Dr Andrews.

45

"Oh, don't go on with that formality. I told you the last time to call me Lily."

Abbey smiled and repeated Lily's name.

"I suppose, as it is not for a court of law, it is okay for me to tell you, even without the full results."

"It appears that the cause of the death is the gash in his stomach. It appears to be a werewolf bite."

Abbey nodded, relieved that it was a werewolf. Had she really thought that Sirius had been the killer? She really didn't know. Her feelings about him changed every time she met him.

"However," Lily continued, "I can't completely confirm that it was a werewolf bite or merely an injury made to look like a werewolf bite until the toxicology comes back. A werewolf bite will show markers in the report, akin to an allergic reaction, which will confirm the results of the examination."

"That's great, thanks," Abbey said, "I won't assume further until you get the final results."

Lily nodded and offered Abbey some tea. She accepted gratefully, and the other woman made the tea and placed it on the table together with some biscuits.

Abbey took a sip and turned the topic to Sirius. "Have you known Sirius long?" she asked.

"He was here when I arrived nearly forty years ago, but he left for a few years and came back nine or ten years ago," Lily replied.

"Why did he leave?" she asked.

"I don't really know. Some people come here and never leave, like myself, but some come and go." She shrugged. "I have always felt it was a great honour to be invited to Misty Vale. Some have found the haven but have not been allowed to enter."

"But how then did they find it?" Abbey asked.

"Wizards have found it, but not all have been allowed in," Lily said. "I haven't experienced someone being turned away myself," she told her. "But Sirius told me that wizards can feel the pull of the magic even if they are not allowed to enter."

"But would a powerful wizard not be able to use magic to get inside?"

"I believe it would take a very powerful wizard to break through or maybe some very dark magic," Lily said, shaking her head. "Thankfully, it has never happened, and hopefully, it never will. I am glad to say that I have never come across a wizard of the age and power that would be necessary to threaten Misty Vale."

Abbey accepted this. "But Sirius was allowed in," Abbey said. "How well do you know him?" she probed.

Lily shrugged again. "As well as anyone, better than some. He had asked for my help for a couple of residents who had health issues when they arrived."

Abbey frowned.

"You don't seem pleased with my answer." She questioned, "Why don't you tell me what's on your mind?"

Abbey nodded, deciding to just ask the woman her opinion. Tiptoeing around wasn't getting her anywhere. "I only met Sirius for the first time when I found Jimmy's body."

Lily murmured, encouraging her to continue.

"I get the feeling he knows something about what happened to Jimmy, and he is not telling me," she said straight out.

"I met him when I arrived forty-odd years ago. He had already been living here for some time. The impression I received about him was that he is dedicated to the safety of Misty Vale and the freedom of the haven it provides. That impression has not changed in the time since. In my dealings with him, he has always had the interests of others at his core."

Abbey felt her shoulders relax.

"If," the other woman continued, "he does know something about Jimmy's death that he isn't sharing with you, I feel sure that it is because he believes it is in the best interest of Misty Vale to keep the information to himself."

Abbey sighed. If this was the case, then it was unlikely he would reveal the information to her.

Lily tapped her hand. "He may tell what he knows if he feels it will help to identify the killer."

Abbey relaxed back in the chair. Lily moved on to chat about the village and query as to what friends and acquaintances they had in common. Abbey drank her tea and ate the biscuits, happy in the relaxed atmosphere of the warm kitchen. She stayed for a good hour until she noticed it was starting to turn dark and thanked the other woman for the information and the nice chat. Lily bid her goodnight with a promise of letting her have the results of the autopsy as soon as she had them.

Abbey walked home at a brisk pace. She thought her only avenue was to visit the bar again the next evening in the hopes of learning more about Jimmy.

Chapter 7

Abbey had managed to rope Lydia into joining her at the bar the next night. Abbey already felt tired when they had sat down with their drinks at the table. Her days and nights since the discovery of Jimmy's body had started to blur into each other. She was burning the candle at both ends, and her sleep, when it came, was plagued by nightmares. The bartenders were a male and a female she had not met before. Abbey had suggested to Lydia that she introduce herself and ask about Jimmy.

Lydia advised her that there was not much point as both had not been in Misty Vale long. The male was a witch, Lydia had told her, and the female was a vampire. Abbey had learned that witches and wizards were not indicators of gender but of the type of magic the person controlled. Witches dealt with medicinal magic and potions. Wizard's magic worked on the physical world.

Abbey sipped at her drink, non-alcoholic. She could not face drinking alcohol today. They had ordered food at the bar, and Abbey hoped that Sarah would be their cook and server.

"Well, you cannot now deny that you are a regular," said a sardonic voice.

Abbey found herself unsurprised to see Sirius.

"Hello, Sirius," she replied, "I see you are also here again, so it seems we are both becoming frequent visitors."

He gave her a half smile, raising one eyebrow. "I think it likely that we are both drawn here for similar reasons."

Abbey agreed and invited him to join them. He sat down and said hello to Lydia. Lydia and Sirius spoke politely for a couple of minutes to each other. This conversation was interrupted only by the arrival of the food that Abbey and Lydia had ordered.

Sarah arrived at the table, and Abbey was happy to see her serving, but she had wished they could have spoken before Sirius arrived.

"Hello, Sarah," Sirius spoke before Abbey could. "I hope that this evening finds you well?" he asked, his voice soft.

The young woman blushed a light pink. "I am, thank you," she replied, placing the food on the table without checking who had ordered which dish. Her attention completely on Sirius.

"Should that male give you any more trouble, know that I am here. You can call on my help at any time." Abbey felt an unwelcome sensation in her chest at Sirius's words to the younger woman.

Sarah thanked him again, and her blush turned a darker red.

Abbey thought it best to insert herself into the conversation before Sarah left the table. "How are you holding up?" she asked.

She turned her eyes towards Abbey. "I am okay, thank you," she said. "Jimmy was more than a boss; he was a friend." Tears filled Sarah's eyes, and she wiped them away. "Have you found out anything else about who attacked Jimmy?" she asked.

Abbey cast a look at Sirius. Lily had sent her a message today confirming that the toxicology was consistent with a werewolf bite. She was sure that Sirius would have received the same message. She didn't think that it was a good idea to tell Sarah this while she was working. The young woman was already so fragile that Abbey felt it best not to tell her until they were in private and with Bill present. She hoped that Sirius would agree.

"No further news at the moment," she said, touching Sarah's hand. "I won't stop until I know the truth." Looking at Sirius, she changed that to, "We won't stop until we find out who did this to Jimmy." Sarah gave her a sad smile, tears still visible in her eyes.

"I know I shouldn't be thinking of myself, but what happens now? I mean, what happens to the bar? This was Jimmy's home. It's not mine and," she said, turning her eyes to Bill, "it's not Bill's. What will happen to the bar?"

"Misty Vale protects its residents. That's its magic," Sirius reassured her. "It will recognise that the bar is home to Bill and you, and it will choose a new owner in time."

"Thank you. I know I should be only thinking of Jimmy, but I was so worried," Sarah said.

"Can you think of anything that might help us to investigate?" Abbey asked.

"No, well maybe," Sarah stuttered.

Abbey nodded in encouragement.

"He was worried, distracted, the night before…" Sarah trailed off without finishing.

"Worried?" Sirius asked.

"Yes, he said something was wrong, but he didn't say what it was. He left the bar before closing time. He said he had to tell someone. I don't know what he thought was wrong, and I don't know who he wanted to tell." Sarah shrugged. "I'm not sure that helps?" she asked.

Abbey thought it was suspicious, but she didn't know what it meant. "I'm sure it does help," Sirius replied. Abbey looked at him, surprised at this. She noticed Sarah relaxing, and she wondered if Sirius had said that merely to reassure her.

"It is so sad. She was obviously really fond of him," Lydia said. After Sarah had excused herself to get back to work.

"Yes," Abbey said, taking a chip from her plate and eating it. Sirius reached over to her plate and snatched a chip. "Hands off," she said.

"But I'm hungry," he replied.

"Order some for yourself," Abbey told him.

"I can't."

"Why not? Don't you have any money?" she asked facetiously.

Sirius raised an eyebrow at her. "I can't ask Sarah to come back to the table so soon after we have upset her, talking about Jimmy," he replied.

Abbey nodded, and with a sigh, she moved her plate with the chips to the middle of the table. She still had her hamburger, after all.

Lydia smiled, passing Sirius a piece of garlic bread from her serving. He smiled at Lydia, and they ate, conversing lightly about the village and the weather. They continued this conversation until they had all finished eating.

"How do you know that about the magic of Misty Vale and the bar?" Abbey asked Sirius.

"I have been resident here for a long time. I have seen the owner of the bar change before."

Abbey nodded. That made sense.

"You received Lily's message about the autopsy results?" Sirius asked.

"Yes," Abbey replied.

Sirius looked at Lydia. "Abbey told me the results," she told him.

"Werewolf," Abbey said, "do you think that young wolf, Jeff, was involved?" she asked.

"He is an aggressive young male, but Jimmy was not too old and one of the strongest wolves I have ever met. Unless he surprised Jimmy, I can't see him being able to best him," Sirius answered.

"Adrenaline can give an increase in strength?" Lydia queried.

Sirius nodded. "Yes, that's true, but even with an adrenaline rush, I don't think it would be enough to match Jimmy," he said.

"I can't see it being Jeff," Abbey confirmed. "He was all bravado when you intervened, but it seemed to me that was all for show."

"That assessment would fit with his place in the clan. He is not a high-ranking wolf," Sirius replied.

"I know Jimmy and Bill were not part of the clan. Are there any other wolves in Misty Vale who are not in the clan?"

"Only Sean. He is the oldest wolf in Misty Vale, and not only would he be unable to take on Jimmy, also he would have no interest. He rarely changes into his wolf form, which is distinctive because of his grey main, but he generally is only interested in his books," Sirius informed them.

"Well, that leaves only the clan wolves," Abbey replied.

"Yes," Sirius responded. "I will visit the clan tomorrow. Would you like to accompany me?" he asked Abbey.

Abbey was surprised by the invitation but readily agreed. They set a time, and Sirius ate the last of the chips and excused himself, agreeing to collect Abbey from her home the following afternoon.

"He seems as eager as you to find Jimmy's killer," Lydia observed.

"Yes," Abbey agreed. "It seems I have been suspicious of him for no reason. It is just that he was there when I came through the mist." Abbey hesitated before continuing, "I haven't told anyone else this, but the night or rather early morning after I found Jimmy, I saw him coming from the bar," she said.

"So," Lydia replied, "he was having a drink."

"No, he told me he hadn't been here when I questioned him last night. Also, it was long after the bar had closed."

"That is interesting," Lydia said.

"I know he is up to something, and I intend to find out what."

Chapter 8

Abbey woke early the next day, or rather, she woke numerous times during the night and the last time she decided to get up. Yawning, she made herself a strong cup of coffee. Her night had been filled with nightmares, and they were still haunting her. She kept dreaming about finding Jimmy's body. She woke the first time from a nightmare where she found the body, and he opened his eyes and told her to find his killer. The next one, Jimmy, in werewolf form, attacked her on the beach of Ballybunion.

She finished her coffee and reached for the pot to pour another one. She went into the living room to retrieve her notebook. Bringing it back to the kitchen, she took a mouthful of coffee, opening to her notes. She read; why dump the body? Who would want to kill Jimmy? What did Jimmy know or do that got him killed? She sighed in frustration; she didn't know the answer to any of the questions. So much for her investigation! What did she know?

A wolf murdered Jimmy. The wolves at the bar seemed to be genuinely in mourning at his loss. She agreed with Sirius's assessment of Jeff. She had to believe that she hadn't met the murderer, yet. Hopefully, meeting with the clan today would give her some leads.

Sirius's willingness to include her in the meeting made her think he, likewise, was not having much luck in his investigation. She drank the rest of her second cup of coffee, still yawning.

She went to get washed and dressed, deciding to go for a walk and have breakfast later.

Sirius collected her at noon, driving a different car to the one he had driven before. "You have more than one car?" Abbey asked.

"The other car was borrowed," he replied. "You do not have a car in Misty Vale?" he asked.

"It is too expensive to have my car brought here. Also, I have only one car, so I need it more for outside of Misty Vale than I need it here." Sirius nodded understanding.

When Abbey had first arrived, she had wondered how the cars got to Misty Vale. Lydia had told her that any large items were transported by the wizards for a charge. It took lots of magic to transport a car, so most people did without and just borrowed one when needed. But the wizards transported anything essential at a much more reasonable charge. Abbey thought that it was funny that magic was used as a delivery service!

"I suppose that wouldn't be a problem for you?" she asked.

Sirius agreed.

They arrived at the clan woods. Sirius parked his car, and they started to hike. "The clan leader is Kane. His home is at the boundary of the clan's lands," Sirius told her.

Kane was standing on his veranda when they arrived. He did not look surprised to see them, and Abbey was sure he had smelled them coming. It was a bit disconcerting. He was frowning. He did not look happy to see them. "What brings you to clan land?" he asked.

"You heard that Jimmy was murdered?" Sirius replied.

"Yes," he answered.

"Dr Andrews carried out an autopsy, and we have received the results," Sirius told him. "A werewolf killed him."

Kane sighed. "You best come inside," he said.

It was obvious that the wolf knew who Sirius was. Abbey had started to notice that everyone seemed to know who Sirius was. He introduced her to the wolf and told him that she had been the one who found Jimmy's body. He had nodded at this information, and it was clear he had already known about her. She wondered if it had been Belinda who had told him. It didn't really matter if she had. Misty Vale was a small place. There were only a couple of hundred residents. Everyone would soon know that it had been her who had found him.

Kane walked inside, and they followed. He opened a cupboard, took out a bottle of whiskey, poured himself a glass, and threw it back. He then turned and offered them a drink. They both refused.

"If he was killed by one of my wolves, then he deserved it. He was always pushing his way into clan business," he said sneeringly.

Abbey was surprised at the dislike in his voice. Everyone so far had spoken well of Jimmy. Yes, they had said he was aggressive but that it stemmed from a protective instinct. But Kane sounded like he was glad Jimmy was gone.

59

"Was there anything that might help to identify which wolf?" he asked.

"No," Sirius replied. "Is there anything you can tell us that might help?"

"Jimmy had some problems with some of the clan wolves," Kane admitted. "I know he recently had a run-in with a young wolf who was making a nuisance of himself."

"Jeff," Abbey supplied.

Kane looked surprised she knew about Jeff, but he nodded in agreement.

"Yes," Kane replied.

"He is a suspect, but there is some doubt that he would have the strength to take on Jimmy," Sirius said.

Kane sighed and nodded. "Ah, I see."

Kane put his hand up to his chin, his eyes looked up to the left. "There are a couple of wolves who would be strong enough to take Jimmy on. Who had had issues with him in the past? Jimmy had run-ins with a lot of clan wolves. I chose not to intervene..." He hesitated. "I am not my wolves' parent; I do not fight their battles for them," Kane told them. He suggested they make themselves comfortable, saying that he would return.

Abbey sat down on a leather couch, and Sirius took a seat beside her. They didn't speak, and Abbey was glad to just sit quietly with her thoughts.

Kane returned with two large males. He introduced a tall blond male as Padraic and the dark-haired male as Richard. Both wolves had scowls on their faces.

Sirius went to speak, but Abbey placed a hand on his arm, silencing him. He acquiesced.

Abbey stood and approached Kane and the two other wolves. She introduced herself.

"I don't know if you are aware of this, but I found Jimmy's body two days ago. Dr Andrews carried out an autopsy, and she has now confirmed that a wolf murdered Jimmy."

"There is no law in Misty Vale," Padraic intoned, "and what happens between wolves is no business of yours. You are only a normal."

"The haven of Misty Vale is the business of all residents," Sirius said. "What Miss Williams failed to mention is that she found Jimmy's body not in Misty Vale but on the beach at Ballybunion."

Padraic shrugged.

Abbey didn't see Richard's reaction, but it wasn't important because Kane growled and Padraic's shoulders slumped in on themselves.

"You both had disagreements with Jimmy. Perhaps you could tell us what those were?" Abbey asked.

"I didn't kill him," Padraic denied, his voice a pitch higher than it had been previously.

"I didn't kill him either," Richard said, sounding bored.

"And what dispute did you have with Jimmy?" Abbey asked.

Richard shrugged. "I got into a fight with a vampire at the bar, he kicked me out. I was still

61

irritated the next day, and I went back to have it out with him. He bruised me up quite badly, but that was the end of it."

Abbey turned to Padraic. "The same," he said.

Kane sighed in frustration. "The truth," he told Padraic.

"I was trying to get Sarah to come back to the clan. He didn't take kindly to it. He told me not to come back to the bar again. I haven't been back since."

"And you haven't bothered Sarah since?" Abbey asked. "We will be checking with Sarah," she informed him.

"I may have asked her to come back to the clan since, but I don't think she told Jimmy it was not in the bar. We didn't fight, he told me to leave, and I left."

"Do either of you have an alibi for the night he was murdered?" she asked.

"They were both with the clan for the night and into the morning," Kane told her. "Richard, in particular, was in no condition to do much but sleep off the alcohol he had drank."

"I didn't kill Jimmy," Padraic interrupted.

Kane turned his eyes to the heavens. "Do you have any other questions?"

"Are either of you aware of any other wolves who had problems with Jimmy?" Sirius asked.

"Jeff," Padraic said.

Sirius nodded.

"Anything else?" Kane asked.

Abbey, looking at Sirius, answered, "No."

Kane told the wolves they could go. "I don't think there is anything else I can tell you," Kane said. "Jimmy was a hot head, and he went up against someone stronger than him, and he paid the price."

Sirius pulled up at Abbey's home. "Kane really didn't like Jimmy," Abbey said.

"No," Sirius agreed.

"Should we put him on the suspect list?" Abbey suggested.

Sirius raised one eyebrow. "There's a list?" he asked.

"There is now," Abbey replied.

"I will let you know if I think of any other avenue for further investigation," Sirius said. And Abbey got out of the car.

Abbey knew Sirius knew something he wasn't telling her, and she was getting nowhere investigating the wolves. Going to the bar every night wasn't giving her any leads. If Sirius was investigating without her, she would follow him to find out what he was up to.

The problem with this plan was that, firstly, she didn't know where he lived, and secondly, she didn't have a car. She decided to stake out the bar that night to see if he turned up again. But she would need a car. Belinda might be willing to let her use her car for the night.

Chapter 9

Abbey wrapped the blanket around her shoulders. Staking out a bar in Ireland in the early hours of the morning in April was cold and boring. It hadn't been boring at first. She had felt like a private detective watching for her quarry as she saw the customers leaving. But then, it had gotten quiet, and the village had been dark and deserted. She had started to feel afraid and foolish.

Someone had just been murdered, and here she was, sitting in a car in the dark. She was not some werewolf or vampire or wizard. She was only a normal human. If even Jimmy could not protect himself, what chance did she have! She had worked herself up to such a state that she had almost left.

But then she thought, yes, Jimmy had been murdered. But it had not been inside Misty Vale. She had started to relax as nothing had happened for more than an hour. Now she was just cold and bored.

Earlier, Belinda had driven the car to the village and handed her the keys. Thankfully, the car was black and blended easily into the shadows. Abbey had parked it down and across from the bar.

She reached for the flask of coffee she had brought with her and poured herself another cup. She decided this would have to be her last cup, as she was not using the alleyway as a bathroom. She sighed for the millionth time.

Finishing her coffee, she put the cup on the floor on the other side of the car. Then she saw it, a shadow, approaching the bar. Was it Sirius? She wasn't sure. She quickly unwrapped herself from the blanket and opened the car door. She climbed out, closing the door softly. She didn't lock the car because if she did, it would make the beeping sound, which would alert her prey that she was following them.

She crossed over to the bar side of the road. She walked softly, thankful that she had changed into her trainers. The male went down the side of the bar, walking under the light. Abbey sighed in relief; it was Sirius. It might have been another man; it might even have been Bill coming home.

Abbey peeped down the side of the bar. Sirius uttered some words, magic, she supposed. He reached for the handle of the side door and opened it. He stepped inside. Abbey sprinted down to the side entrance, afraid the door would relock behind him. The door closed before she reached it. Abbey grasped the handle and took a deep breath. It opened for her. She stepped inside.

It was dark in the bar, but the light from the moon and the street lighting was enough to illuminate the bar. There was no sign of Sirius. If he had gone upstairs, Abbey didn't think she could follow. The chances of either Sarah or Bill catching her were too high. Sirius had magic. Maybe he could turn himself invisible. Abbey didn't have anything to hide herself with. Abbey looked at the door to the kitchen. Hopefully, he went that way.

She crept into the kitchen, expecting at any moment that Sirius would discover her. The kitchen was completely black. She couldn't see Sirius. There were no windows to brighten the space, but at the far end, in the ground, there was a faint light. Abbey inched towards the light, probing with her hands to feel for any obstacles. She reached the point of the light in the ground. The light came from a hole in the floor.

Abbey looked down; she could see the top of Sirius's head. He stood over a glowing yellow light, his hands outstretched, and he was mumbling. She couldn't hear the words and doubted that they would be in English even if she could. She tiptoed backwards, away from the hole, being careful not to disturb anything.

She reached the kitchen door, glancing behind her to be sure Sirius hadn't seen her. She didn't think it would be a good idea for him to find her here. She closed the kitchen door gently and moved quickly to the unlocked side door. She opened it, slinked out and closed it quietly behind her. Then she dashed up the side of the bar and back to the car. Without turning on the lights, she drove away.

She didn't take a deep breath until she had parked the car in front of her house. Once she had parked the car and switched off the engine, she let her head drop to the steering wheel.

What had Sirius been doing? She knew he had been hiding something from her. Had she been too quick to accept Lily's word about Sirius and the autopsy? She didn't know the doctor any better than she knew Sirius. Lily's loyalty would lay with Sirius, whom she knew better than she knew Abbey, whom she had only met. It would explain why trying to find a wolf with a reason to kill Jimmy was getting her nowhere. But then why would Sirius have bothered to bring Jimmy's body to Lily in the first place. Abbey hadn't known Lily and wouldn't have even thought that there was anyone in Misty Vale who could perform an autopsy!

She got out of the car and went into her house. She knew she should try to work this out, but her brain was too tired. The adrenaline of fearing that Sirius would catch her following him into the bar, together with the night spent in the car, had caught up with her. She dragged herself to her bedroom, readied herself for bed, and was asleep the moment her head hit the pillow.

She didn't wake until late; it was nearly lunchtime. Thankfully, she didn't have to work that day. She was feeling more rational now that she had slept. She was determined not to jump to any conclusions. Abbey didn't know what Sirius had been doing in the bar. She didn't know enough about magic. Sirius being in the bar did not mean he had killed Jimmy. She would include Sirius on her suspect list. But she would still take advantage of any contacts he had that might help her. He was now a suspect, but he was not the only suspect. Every wolf in Misty Vale would be suspect as well.

She was going to go back to the beginning and start with Jimmy himself. When had he arrived in Misty Vale? How had he come to be the owner of the bar, and for the matter, who was McCafferty? And where was he?

All the wolves in Misty Vale were suspect, including the clan wolves, even wolves who had not had issues with Jimmy. She would investigate any wolf whom she could find had any connection with Jimmy. She would also be looking closer at Bill and Sarah. One of them might now become the owner of the bar. Was that reason enough for murder?

And finally, she would consider Sirius and his connection with Jimmy, his connection with the bar. She would also have to find out more about magic. She needed to know what magics Sirius might have been doing in the bar last night.

Abbey had been running around in circles, and it had been getting her nowhere. She had heard previously that the vampires were the custodians of the history of Misty Vale. She needed to approach the vampires to find out about the bar and more about Jimmy's past. The only problem was that she didn't really know any vampires well enough that she could ask them.

Sirius had introduced her to Tobias. Could she ask him? He was a friend of Sirius;' she would have to be careful. She would have to keep her request for information general. And pretend her questions had nothing to do with the murder but only interest in what would happen to the bar. There was only one problem with this plan. She had no idea where the vampire lived. She would have to see if Lydia knew where the vampire's home was.

Chapter 10

It was late afternoon when Abbey pulled the car up to Tobias's home. She had spoken to Lydia earlier, and Lydia had been able to supply directions to his house. It was on the most westerly side of Misty Vale, and Abbey was glad she hadn't needed to walk. She had rung Belinda earlier, who had agreed to let Abbey hold on to the car for another day. She had expected a gothic mansion. She shrugged to herself as she parked the car in front of a traditional Irish thatched cottage. Tobias was in the garden, and he looked over when she got out of the car.

He gave her a quizzical smile. "I did not expect to meet you again so soon?"

"Hi," Abbey replied, "I thought I would take advantage of the introduction to pick your brain."

Tobias reached for a cloth at his feet, wiping his hands. Abbey's mouth dropped open; she became aware that she had interrupted his gardening! Tobias smiled, recognising the disbelief on her face. "You really are new to this world," he said. "Do you expect me to be a beast, unable to control my blood lust? Am I meant to be sculking in the dark, afraid of the sunlight?" he asked.

Abbey shrugged and smiled, slightly self-conscious. "I have learnt a little since I arrived in Misty Vale, but I must admit that the stories from the normal world are still with me." Abbey hoped that the vampire was not insulted by her admitted ignorance.

He laughed. "Come inside," he said. "I have some lemonade in the fridge."

Abbey put her hand up to cover her mouth, smothering a laugh. Tobias smiled at her again. Even though the laugh hadn't escaped, Abbey got the feeling he knew she thought the invitation was funny. She thanked him and followed him inside. He directed her to sit at the table in the small, bright kitchen and got her a glass of lemonade and one for himself from the fridge.

When he poured the second glass of lemonade, Abbey was glad that Tobias hadn't seen her face. She had assumed that vampires only drank blood, and now she was questioning everything she thought she knew.

He sat down across from her at the table. "What can I help you with?" he asked.

"I was thinking about the bar," she said.

He nodded, encouraging her to continue.

"I wondered what will happen to the bar now that Jimmy's gone. And then I was wondering why it is named McCafferty's? Jimmy's name was not McCafferty?"

"You are aware that vampires are historians," he said, "but why did you choose me as your source?"

"Yes, I had heard that vampires are the keepers of the history of Misty Vale. I would like to say that I believed you were the most knowledgeable, but the truth is, you are the only vampire I have been introduced to," she admitted.

71

Tobias laughed. "Well, there goes my vanity," he said. "McCafferty was the name of the original owner of the bar. He came here in the early twentieth century until he died in the nineteen seventies. The next owner was," Tobias paused, putting his hand up to his chin. "Paul Kelly," he said. "Paul died ten years ago," he said, nodding. "Jimmy arrived immediately, and the bar claimed him as its new owner."

"Paul died?" she asked, her voice rising with her eyebrows.

"Yes," Tobias replied.

"How did he die?" she asked.

"He was murdered," Tobias told her.

"Murdered!" Abbey said, her voice so high-pitched it was almost a squeak. Abbey was wondering why no one had mentioned this before. The previous owner of the bar had been murdered as well. Abbey recalled that there had not been a murder in Misty Vale in ten years. She now knew that the murder victim had been Paul Kelly.

"Why did Sirius not mention that the previous owner of the bar had also been murdered?" Abbey asked. "Surely, the person who murdered Paul would be a suspect in Jimmy's murder?"

"Paul was a werewolf. The person who murdered him was a vampire. The vampire came to see me after he murdered Paul. He told me that he had lost control of himself," Tobias said. "You must understand, whatever your books might have told you, it is not common for vampires to lose control.

"Also, we do not feed on werewolves. He told me he blacked out, and when he came back to himself, Paul was dead at his feet. He was inconsolable. Paul had been his friend. He wanted me to kill him. He could not forgive himself. I refused, but I felt that the decision should not be just for the vampires. I consulted with Sirius. He did not believe that death was the answer. Sirius used his magic and barred the vampire from ever entering Misty Vale or any other haven again. You will comprehend from this that he is not a suspect in Jimmy's murder."

"But," Abbey said, "Jimmy's body was not found in Misty Vale."

"No, but having seen the young vampire after murdering Paul and his willingness to die for the crime, I feel confident that he would never commit such a heinous act again."

Abbey sighed, nodding, swayed by Tobias's confidence.

"Moreover, I understand that Jimmy was murdered by a wolf?" he queried.

"Yes," Abbey admitted, shaking her head. "So, what happens to the bar now that Jimmy has been murdered?"

"The bar will select a new owner," he told her.

"Does anyone know how the bar does that?" Abbey asked.

Tobias laughed. "It is not so much that the bar selects a new owner," he clarified. "It is truer to say that Misty Vale will select a new owner. The bar is only a building. As to how that happens." Tobias shrugged. "How does Misty Vale provide the perfect home for each of its residents?"

Abbey shook her head. "Magic," she said.

"Magic," Tobias repeated.

"So, no one could know in advance that they would be the next owner of the bar?" she asked.

"I don't believe so, but Sirius would know more about the magic of Misty Vale than I."

Abbey had driven back to the village, wondering if that was what Sirius had been doing in the bar. Was he trying to interfere with the magic of Misty Vale to ensure that Sarah got to keep her home at the bar? Abbey couldn't help but think that it was too much of a coincidence that the previous owner of the bar had also been murdered. She needed to find out more about what transpired ten years ago. Lily had said that Sirius had returned to Misty Vale ten years ago.

Tobias said he consulted with him after Paul's murder. But had he arrived back before or after Paul had been murdered. Lydia had been here at the time. Abbey wondered if she knew when Sirius had arrived back. She needed to know what relationship Sirius had with Jimmy. She also had to learn more about magic if she wanted to know what Sirius had been up to.

She started with dropping into the diner to talk to Lydia. Luckily, the diner was quiet, with only one person drinking coffee and no one waiting to be served.

"I'm glad you decided to drop in," Lydia said before Abbey could speak. "Carter," she said, pointing to the only customer, "told me something interesting," Lydia told her.

"What did he tell you?" Abbey asked.

Lydia started walking towards Carter, beckoning Abbey to come with her. "Carter," she said when they arrived at his table, "this is Abbey, the woman I said was investigating Jimmy's murder," she reminded him.

"Oh, yes," Carter said.

He was a slightly built male, and he looked to be no more than twenty-five, but Abbey had learnt in her time in Misty Vale that looks could be deceiving. She was sure that the male was not a werewolf, but other than that, she wasn't sure. He was not very beautiful. His features were too sharp for that. But there was something ethereal about him. He had blond hair and deep green eyes.

"I was telling Lydia that I saw Jimmy after the bar had closed the night before you found his body," the male told her.

Abbey gasped. This was what she needed: someone who knew Jimmy's movements before he had been murdered.

"I was making my way home," he said. "Jimmy came towards me from the direction of Sirius's home. He seemed worried," Carter said. "I asked him if he was okay and if there was anything I could help him with. He said no, but in such a distracted way that I wondered if he had heard me at all. I wouldn't have thought any

75

further about it until I heard that he had been murdered." The male raised both his hands upwards. "That's it," he said. "I don't know if that helps?"

"Thank you," Abbey said. "I'm sure it does. Anything that can tell us his state of mind has to be useful."

The male nodded and picked up his coffee. Abbey didn't think there was any point in questioning him further, so she left him to drink his coffee in peace.

"Lydia," Abbey said. "Do you know about Paul Kelly, the previous owner of the bar, having been murdered too?" she asked.

"Yes, sorry, I had actually forgotten about that," Lydia replied, her forehead crinkling. "Do you think they are related?"

"I don't know, but Lily told me that Sirius had been away from Misty Vale for some years previously and had only returned ten years ago. Do you know if Sirius returned before Paul was murdered or after?" she asked.

Lydia put one hand up to her head, and her mouth twisted. "I'm sorry, Abbey, I don't remember if he was here before or just after. I wish I could be more help."

"Don't worry, it is not important, and it is probably only a coincidence that both Jimmy and Paul had owned the bar. The nature of the two murders sounds very different, and Tobias told me that the vampire who killed Paul confessed."

"That's right," Lydia said. "Simon, he was truly a very lovely male, and everyone was shocked that he had lost control. In fact, if he hadn't admitted to the murder, I wouldn't have believed it."

Abbey thought that it was sad that the vampire had lost control and murdered his friend. Had something similar happened with Jimmy? Had Jimmy been murdered by someone he considered a friend!

Abbey shook the thought away. "There is something you can help me with," she said. "I am wondering if you have any books on magic?" Abbey asked.

Lydia's eyebrows raised at this question. "You know that you won't be able to learn magic?" she asked.

Abbey laughed. "Yes, I know I won't be able to learn how to do magic. I was just curious about how magic works," she said. "If that makes sense?"

Lydia smiled. "The answer is yes, I do have some books on magic, even a couple written by witches or wizards. I will have a look at my books at home this evening and bring a couple in for you to borrow," she promised.

Happy with this promise, Abbey said goodbye and drove out to Belinda to return the car. The information that Carter had given her was in line with what Sarah had said about Jimmy being concerned about something and that he had to tell someone. Was that someone Sirius? Had Jimmy visited Sirius just before he had been murdered? Had he spoken to Sirius?

She would also ask Belinda about Sarah and Bill. They were the wolves closest to Jimmy. There was no point in coming up with some grand theory involving Paul's murder ten years earlier before she had fully considered a simpler explanation.

Chapter 11

Belinda opened the front door before Abbey had climbed from the car. "Are you staying for coffee?" she called.

"Yes, thanks," Abbey replied, handing her the keys.

"How has the investigation been going?" Belinda asked.

"The car was very useful, thank you. I now know that Sirius is up to something. I waited near the bar, and he was there again after it had closed and all the lights had gone off. He unlocked the side door and let himself in. I followed him. There is something in the ground in the kitchen of the bar. He was performing magic over it. I got out before he saw me, but I want to know what he was doing."

Belinda brought her hand to her mouth. "Oh my, what is he up to?"

Abbey shook her head. "I don't know, but I can't think about it right now. What I want to do is find out more about Bill and Sarah."

"I know Sarah quite well. She grew up in Misty Vale," Belinda responded. "She came here with her father when she was about ten years old. They were part of the clan. Her father left without her when she was about seventeen. She was happy with the clan until she turned nineteen and Jeff arrived in Misty Vale. He was sweet with her at first. I think he thought she was just playing hard to get. But when she didn't come round, he got more persistent."

79

Abbey shook her head, thinking about how hard it must have been for the young woman.

"She could have gone to Kane," Belinda said.

"Yes, Kane," Abbey said, and Belinda raised her eyebrows. She had heard the question in Abbey's words.

"When Sirius and I visited Kane, he didn't seem to be unhappy about Jimmy's death," Abbey said.

Belinda shrugged. "They were not friends," she explained. "Kane probably thinks that Jimmy intervened in clan business when he should have stayed away. Kane's job will be easier with Jimmy gone," Belinda confirmed. "But Kane is a good male. He would never have murdered Jimmy," Belinda said.

"But if he was such a good male, why didn't he protect Sarah from Jeff?" Abbey asked.

"I think he didn't realise how far it had gone. He didn't know how fearful Sarah had become," Belinda said. "I know Kane would have intervened, but he was too slow, so instead, Sarah went to Jimmy."

"So, you don't think Sarah would have hurt Jimmy or Jimmy would have done anything to make her murder him?" Abbey asked.

"I can't see it," she said. "I saw them together, and although he was probably only twenty years older than her, he was fatherly towards her. Also, while she had a home in the bar, I don't think she needed to own it. The businesses in Misty Vale are hardly gold mines," she said, laughing.

Abbey nodded. "What about Bill?"

"I really don't know much about him. He arrived about two years ago. Although he is in his forties, he is a very strong wolf. Kane told me that he approached him when he arrived to join the clan, but Bill said no. He could be a clan leader. He is that strong, so I was surprised Kane had invited him to join the clan. I think some of the tension between Kane and Jimmy was because Jimmy was also strong enough to be clan leader. Maybe that's why he invited Bill to join. Maybe he hoped if Bill was a clan wolf, he wouldn't have to deal with him interfering in clan business the way Jimmy did."

Abbey bobbed her head. "There would be more clout in being clan leader than in owning the bar."

Belinda agreed, "It always seemed to me that Bill had some bad history. A wolf that strong he must have spent his whole life fighting. Everyone would want to test against him. I think he wasn't interested in being clan leader because he had nothing to prove. I think he came here for the quiet life, and that's what Jimmy gave him."

"Jimmy turned the bar into its own mini haven," Abbey said.

"Yes, all the staff have gone to him because they needed a family. That's what he gave them."

She would go back to the bar tonight and talk more to Bill and Sarah. They must have gotten over the worst of the shock of Jimmy's death by now and might be more open to talking. Maybe they knew something about the bar and might even know what it was that Sirius was doing. But she would have to be careful what she said. She didn't want to tell them Sirius had been performing magic in the bar if it might put him in danger. She didn't know if the magic Sirius had done was protective or malicious.

Abbey walked into the bar at opening time. She wanted to talk to Sarah and Bill before the other customers arrived. Bill and Sarah were both behind the bar when she got there. Bill nodded to her, and Sarah gave her a small smile.

"Hi," Abbey said.

Bill grunted, and Sarah said "hi" back.

"How are you doing, Sarah?" she asked.

"I'm okay. Bill has been so kind."

Bill looked over at her and patted her on the shoulder.

"Have you got the autopsy report?" Bill asked.

"No, but," Abbey hesitated, "Lily confirmed that it was a wolf bite."

Sarah wiped at her eyes.

Bill nodded. "I need a copy of the report," he said.

Abbey wasn't sure if there was a report. Why would Lily do a report? It wasn't like they could bring the crime to the Guards. Maybe Lily had done a report. She would ask her in the morning. "I will get you a copy," she said.

"Sirius told us Jimmy's body will be available tomorrow. We are having a wake for him," Sarah said. "Will you come?"

Abbey nodded, and Sarah told her the details. "I will be here," Abbey said.

"In the meantime, can I ask a few questions?" she asked.

"Anything that will help to find out who killed him," Sarah replied.

"I noticed there was a different bartender on the other night?" she questioned.

"Yes, Stephane," Bill replied. "He is a young vampire. He lives with a couple of other vampires, but he does an odd shift here. More shifts now that Jimmy is gone; we need the help," he said.

"Are there any other staff?" Abbey asked.

"Marina," Sarah answered, "she helps out in the kitchen. She is a witch. She is very shy, so she doesn't work front of house."

Abbey's eyebrows raised at this information, for Sarah, whom Abbey had thought to be shy to describe someone else that way. The poor woman must be painfully shy that she wouldn't even come out of the kitchen.

"Did they have a good relationship with Jimmy?" she asked.

Bill shook his head at this question. "Jimmy was a good employer. Everyone who worked for him had a good relationship with him," he said.

"Sirius has been so helpful in trying to find Jimmy's murder," Abbey said.

"Yes, he has been so kind," Sarah replied. "He has been checking up on us to make sure we are okay."

"He was probably close with Jimmy?" she asked.

"Not close, but he did used to pop in sometimes, and they would sit down and have a chat," Sarah said. "Never while the bar was open, just kind of neighbourly," she explained.

Now that was interesting, Abbey thought. He had definitely implied that he barely knew Jimmy.

"You said before that Jimmy seemed worried about something?" Abbey asked Sarah.

"Yes," Sarah replied, "he did seem worried."

"Do you have any idea what he might have been worried about?"

"No," Sarah answered.

"I wish I did know," said Bill.

The door to the bar opened, and a couple of customers arrived. Abbey thought she should let them get on with their work. She said her goodbyes and left.

Chapter 12

Abbey decided to walk out to Lily's house to ask if there was an autopsy report. She had energy for the first time in days. She had gone straight home after talking to Sarah and Bill the night before. Had cooked herself a nice dinner and had a quiet evening.

After a hot bath, she crawled into bed and slept peacefully all night. It was the first night since finding Jimmy's body that she hadn't been plagued by nightmares.

The sun was high, and it was nearly noon, but it was still April, so there was a little bit of a chill in the air. She grabbed her light coat and set off. Lily's house was only a half-hour walk from her home. She breathed in the fresh air and let herself enjoy the exercise.

She hoped Lily would be home and wouldn't mind her visiting for the second time without an invitation. She could just have called her, but she wanted to talk to her in person. She hoped Lily had done an autopsy report, but if she hadn't, she might ask her to do one. Even though she probably wouldn't be able to understand it enough to get any clues. She wanted to see everything Lily had discovered in one place. If there was a report, she would go on the internet and do some research, which might help her to interpret the findings.

Abbey knocked gently on Lily's door, conscious of her rudeness in turning up uninvited. Lily opened the door immediately. She took a step back at the sight of Abbey on her doorstep. Abbey realised that Lily hadn't heard the knock and, by the fact that she had her coat on, was leaving herself.

"Abbey," she said, her hand at her chest, "you gave me such a fright."

Abbey apologized for the fright and for turning up without checking with her that it was okay. Lily reassured her that it wasn't a problem. She explained that being the only doctor in the village, people often turned up at her door all hours of the day and night.

"Unfortunately, I am on my way out," she said.

"I was only wondering if you had done up an autopsy report on Jimmy?" Abbey asked.

"Yes," she said. "I gave a copy to Sirius. Would you like a copy? I can print you off one?" she offered.

"You are on your way out. I can call another time," Abbey said.

"Not at all. It will only take a couple of minutes. Come on in," the doctor replied.

Abbey followed her into the house, and Lily led her to a little office in the back. She turned on her computer and pressed a few buttons.

"Would you be able to give me a second copy?" Abbey asked. "Bill in the bar asked for it," she explained.

"No problem, dear," Lily replied, and after pressing a few more buttons on the computer, her little printer sprang to life. Lily handed her the two copies. "I would invite you to coffee, but I have a couple of house calls. A doctor's work is never finished," she said.

Abbey thanked her. The doctor waved away her words. Abbey said her goodbyes as Lily got in her little car and drove off in the opposite direction to Abbey's. Abbey clutched the report tightly, not glancing at it, while she walked home. She would read her copy when she got there and give Bill a copy later.

Abbey sat down at her kitchen table; she laid out the report. She started reading: identification of the decedent, description of clothing and personal effects. She skimmed over these parts. Then she came to circumstances of death. This set up the details of how Abbey had found the body. It detailed the description of the photographs and copies of the photos.

Seeing the photographs again brought it all back, and Abbey shuddered. It was horrible, the way he had died. It reiterated Abbey's decision to do everything she could to find Jimmy's murderer. Shaking the feeling off, she went on with reading the report. It then set out Lily's examination and details of the injuries.

Then, it set out the toxicology report details. It finished up with Lily's opinion. It was, as Lily had said, the detail of the injury described the wounds on the stomach and the description of bite marks. It gave estimates of the size of the teeth that inflicted the wounds.

"Oh yuck," Abbey said out loud at the details of the bite marks. She reminded herself that they were not human teeth but wolf teeth. It was still disgusting.

The report finished up with Lily's opinion that the bites were from a werewolf. That the toxicology report bore out this examination due to the toxin found in his blood. The report also detailed some postmortem injuries most likely caused by his body being thrown from the cliff. It also gave the opinion that, given that Jimmy had been found fully clothed, that he had not changed form. The assailant would have been unlikely to have suffered anything but superficial wounds. That was interesting. Why had Jimmy not changed form when he was being attacked?

Abbey didn't have any further time to ponder the report. The wake would be starting soon. She went to her bedroom to get changed and brush her hair. She walked briskly back into town.

The bar was already packed when she walked in. The body lay in a coffin in the centre of the room. On a table beside the coffin was a large glass of whiskey, a plate with rare steak, and a well-read book. They were for Jimmy to bring with him to the afterlife. Someone would stay with the body until burial, guarding him until he was laid to rest.

The whole village appeared to be there, and Abbey joined Lydia and Rick, who were standing off to one side. Sarah and Bill were seated closest to the body. Abbey spotted Belinda, Kane, and a group of other muscular people, whom Abbey thought werewolves, too. The bar was closed for business.

Drinks were lined up at the bar for people to help themselves. There were containers of soup and sandwiches lined up on tables near the bar. Abbey felt eyes on her and looked up to see Sirius and Tobias arrive.

Sirius didn't seem to have noticed her. Abbey's eyes followed him. He left his friend's side and strode over to Sarah. He reached out and took her hand. Abbey could see he was talking to Sarah quietly but intensely. Sarah was hanging on his every word.

"Hello, Abbey."

She had been so focused on watching Sirius and Sarah that she hadn't noticed Tobias approaching her.

"Hello, Tobias, it's lovely to see you again." The vampire smiled softly at her.

"May I join you?" he asked.

"That would be great," she said. Maybe she would get more out of him about Sirius.

The bar fell silent. Bill started telling a story about his first time in the bar. And how Jimmy had stopped a fight between himself, another wolf and a vampire. He laughed as he told how, at the end, the wolf and the vampire had become bosom buddies. Sirius came over to Abbey's table and took a seat between herself and Tobias without asking.

Then Sarah took over from Bill, telling her own story. It continued in that way, with one person taking over from another, telling stories about Jimmy. The stories continued for a time, and then the music started with one person singing and more joining in.

Abbey had started to get tired; it was getting close to the time the bar would normally close. She wasn't a close friend of Jimmy's, and she didn't think she would be expected to stay much longer. Groups of people were talking separately.

Abbey picked up her bag and coat and made for the door.

"May I walk you home," Sirius said from behind her. He had left her table once the stories had finished, and he had joined Sarah again. He hadn't come back, and she had left him alone. She didn't know what to say to him. But maybe he had something to say to her?

"That would be nice," she agreed.

Abbey turned in the direction of her home, walking slowly, and Sirius kept pace with her. "You and Tobias seem to be getting on very well?" he asked.

"Yes," she replied. Tobias had stayed sitting with her for nearly the whole time he had been there, but he had left a couple of hours earlier. She had tried to ask him again about Sirius, but the information he had given her had been no different to that she had received from Lily. They had then spoken about his love of gardening. And how it was a hobby he had only been able to indulge in since he had arrived at Misty Vale. As one of the truths about vampires from the fictional world was that they could not go out in sunlight. However, Misty Vale allowed them the freedom to do so.

Sirius waited to see if Abbey was going to elaborate, and when he saw that she was not, he asked her about how she had adjusted to living in Misty Vale.

Abbey gave a small laugh. "Lydia met me that first day. When she told me what Misty Vale was, I thought either she was crazy or I was." She laughed again. "Or maybe we were both crazy! But I have lived here for a few months now, and even though I am a normal, it feels like home. Why does Misty Vale open for some normals?" she asked.

"No one really knows," he said. "I have always thought that Misty Vale needs something that person has, so it invites them in."

"You have lived here a long time?" she asked, wondering if he would tell her the truth.

Now Sirius laughed. "I don't know if you are aware of the lifespan of the average wizard?" he asked.

"I have heard that most wizards live to be a couple of hundred years?"

Sirius nodded. "I am very old," he replied. "I first came here a long time ago. However, I have come and gone many times since. Most recently, I have come back to Misty Vale, ten years ago."

Abbey recognized that she could use this opening to ask about Paul Kelly's murder, but she didn't. Instead, she asked, "Had your home changed when you came back?" she asked.

"No," he said. "Whenever I come back, my home is exactly as I left it, including the food left there. It remains the same as the day I left Misty Vale."

Abbey shook her head. "The magic is really amazing. Misty Vale is such a wonderful place. A fantasy like I used to read about before I came here." She smiled at him. "I feel so blessed to have been invited here. Whenever I leave, I am always afraid that I won't get back in."

"Once you have been invited, you always have a home here unless you break the rules of the haven. There are not many rules, in fact. There is only one rule I know of, and that is do not take away the haven from others. I do not see that becoming a problem for you." He smiled.

Abbey wondered about Sirius's interest in Sarah. It had not seemed that they knew each other except in passing when Sirius and herself had called to the bar. But Abbey could not deny that Sirius seemed to be paying a lot of attention to the younger woman since then.

Abbey decided it was time to ask Sirius what he was up to. Abbey took a deep breath and let it out. "Why don't you tell me what you were doing at the bar the night after Jimmy was murdered?"

Sirius looked surprised at the question. With a wry smile, he asked, "Have you been following me?"

"No," Abbey replied. "Belinda was dropping me home, and we drove by the bar when you came out."

"I wanted to have a look around to see if there were any clues in Jimmy's personal effects."

Abbey's mouth twisted slightly; she knew this wasn't the real reason. But he didn't know that she had seen him in the kitchen the next time. But at least he hadn't denied being in the bar. "And did you find anything?" she asked.

"No, unfortunately not," he said.

"Then why did you go back to the bar again?" she asked, deciding to be brave.

"So you were following me?" he replied, his tone was curious but not angry.

Abbey shrugged. There was no point in denying it. "Not the first time," she said.

Sirius hesitated to answer. "So I am now on the suspect list?" he asked. "Is it only Kane and I on the list, or have you added any other names?"

Abbey wondered if she had made a mistake telling him that she had followed him. Especially while they were alone. But everyone she had spoken to had only good things to say about Sirius. Abbey decided to tell him the truth. "I followed you into the bar the second time," she admitted.

Sirius's eyebrows raised at this. "If you followed me in, then why are you asking me what I was doing?"

"I don't know magic," she said, raising her hands in the air.

Sirius sighed and then shook his head. She thought he was coming to some decision. He

93

looked straight at her and said, "Misty Vale is built on a well of natural magic."

Abbey nodded to confirm she was listening.

"The source is located under the bar," he said and stopped to see what she thought of this.

"How do you know this?" she asked.

"I am a very old wizard," he replied. "I can feel the magic."

"Okay, and what were you doing in the bar?" she repeated.

"I was checking that the source was safe," he replied.

Abbey had no way to know if this was the truth, but she decided to trust him.

"How is your investigation going?" he asked. "You didn't confirm if it is only Kane and me on the suspect list or if you have added anyone else?"

Abbey shrugged and ignored the question. Instead, she asked, "Why didn't you tell me Lily had given you a copy of the autopsy report?"

"I wasn't aware you had any medical expertise," he said, shaking his head. "I didn't think you would want more than to know it had been a wolf, and Lily informed me that she had already told you this?"

Abbey nodded, accepting his explanation. "I agree that I don't have any medical expertise, but I got a copy of the report from Lily," she said. "The one thing that struck me was that Jimmy had not changed into his wolf?" She wondered what Sirius's view of this would be.

"Yes," he said, "that was surprising."

"Why do you think he didn't change?" she asked.

Sirius put his hand up to his forehead. "There are a number of possible explanations," he said. "One, his attacker surprised him, and he didn't have time to change."

Abbey nodded.

"Another possible reason is that he might have tried to reason with his attacker, which would not be possible in wolf form."

"Why would he try to reason with a wolf who was attacking him? It doesn't seem to fit with his personality. Everyone I have spoken to has said that Jimmy was protective but aggressive," Abbey queried.

"Maybe it was someone he considered a friend," Sirius said. And Abbey knew that she had already been thinking that but had not let herself acknowledge it. Because that brought her back to Bill and Sarah. The two wolves Jimmy would have considered his friends.

"You are thinking that this makes Bill the most likely killer, or Sarah?" Sirius questioned.

"Yes, but their grief seems to be genuine," Abbey said.

"Yes, Sarah, in particular, seemed disconsolate," Sirius agreed.

"Did you see Jimmy before he was murdered?" Abbey asked him.

"Not for some time," he said.

"Sarah said that he had told her he was worried, and he was going to tell someone? Who do you think he would have told something like that to?" Abbey asked.

Sirius looked thoughtful. "I hope it would have been me," he said. "Unfortunately, I was not home that night, as you know," he said.

Abbey shook her head; how would she know he had not been home?

"I met you the next morning coming back through the mist, pulling Jimmy's legs!" he reminded her. Then Sirius stopped walking and surprised Abbey stopped too. He had turned to her, and she looked up at him, her forehead crinkling in query.

"We are here," Sirius said, looking down at her. His eyes suddenly intense, and Abbey found she could not look away. She stood there looking into his eyes for a moment, her brain not understanding what he had said. Then she dragged her eyes away from his and looked around. They had arrived at her home.

"Oh yes," Abbey said, feeling her face warm in a blush that she was glad the darkness hid. "Thank you for walking me home," she said. Before she could step away from him, he bent down a placed a soft kiss on her cheek. Abbey felt her blush deepening.

"Goodnight," she said, rushing towards her door. She didn't turn back or hear if he had said goodnight back as she closed her door behind her.

The burial was early in the morning, with most of the town again turning up at the small village graveyard. It was nondenominational, and the graves were marked only with plaques. A pipe was played during the burial, but no words were spoken. All had been said the night before.

Sarah and Bill came over to her, and they thanked her for coming.

"I was glad to be here," she said.

"How are you both?" she asked.

Sarah shrugged. "I am hoping that after the wake, I will be able to sleep through the night without having nightmares."

"Nightmares?" Abbey asked.

"Yes," Sarah said. "I keep having nightmares that it was me who killed him. I would never do that," she reassured Abbey. "He was like a father to me."

Abbey noticed that Bill did not look shocked at Sarah's nightmares, so she had probably told him before.

"I understand," Abbey said. "I had similar nightmares for a couple of nights after I found his body." Sarah gave her a small smile on hearing this.

"Did you get the report?" Bill asked.

"Oh, yes," Abbey replied, grabbing the report from her bag and handing it to him.

"Thank you," he said, putting it in his back pocket.

They shared a few more words about the night before, and how much Jimmy would have enjoyed the stories, and Bill and Sarah went off to speak to some other people.

Chapter 13

"Jeff has been gravely injured." Abbey opened her door the next morning to find Sirius standing there.

"What?" Abbey said.

"He was found unconscious this morning outside of the bar," Sirius told her.

"You had better come in," Abbey told him. She walked ahead of him into the kitchen. She sat down heavily on one of the chairs by the table, and Sirius took one across from her. "Who found him?" Abbey asked.

"Bill, he found him this morning. He rang me immediately, and I sent Tobias to him," Sirius told her. "Tobias was able to apply his saliva to the wounds to slow down the bleeding while they waited for me to arrive. When I arrived, I placed him in stasis. We have transferred him to Lily's, and she is treating him.

"Does it look like it was another werewolf attack?" she asked.

"No, it appears that his wrist and throat were slit."

Abbey gasped at the horrifying description of the young wolf's injuries.

Sirius looked at her, his eyebrows furrowed in a deep frown, putting his hands up to his face. "It looks like he dragged himself to the bar from the beach."

Abbey covered her mouth with her hands. She had not even met the wolf, and the story of how he had behaved towards Sarah had not endeared him to her. But here was another terrible attack, and from the sound of it, if Bill had not found him when he had, Jeff would have died, too.

"From the beach, was he attacked in Misty Vale or Ballybunion?" she asked.

"There is no way to know until he is recovered enough to tell us," Sirius said.

"Do you think he was trying to get help at the bar?" Abbey asked. "Or do you think his attacker might have been in the bar?"

"Either is possible," Sirius said.

Abbey nodded. This made sense.

"Bill agreed to tell Kane, and I came here," he told her.

"Do you know if Jeff has any family in Misty Vale?" Abbey asked.

"No, he only has the clan," Sirius said.

Abbey shuddered; she no longer felt the safety and peace which Misty Vale had given her when she had arrived here five months ago. One person had been murdered, and now another had been gravely injured, only eight days apart. Who would be next? Anyone who crossed over to Ballybunion was in danger of becoming the next victim.

"You were on your way out?" Sirius asked.

"I have to go to work," Abbey replied.

"You will have a lunch break?" he asked.

"Yes."

"I will call the diner at one, and we can talk during your lunch?" he suggested.

99

"One is the busiest time. Two would be better," she offered.

He agreed, and Abbey got on her bicycle and cycled to work. Her brain was in a tangle. Who was killing off the werewolves of Misty Vale?

Lydia looked at Abbey, her eyebrows raised. Abbey smiled; it was the fifth time Lydia had caught her looking at the clock. At least this time, it was nearly two. The bell on the door of the diner pinged, and Abbey smiled at Sirius as he walked in. Abbey felt herself blush slightly at the sight of him. The news of Jeff's attack this morning had pushed all thought of the scene on her doorstep the night before from her mind. But seeing him now brought it back to her.

Abbey waited for the blush to subside; she was determined not to behave like a teenager with a crush just because he had kissed her cheek! Abbey picked up a menu and walked over to meet him.

"If you want to choose something, I will pass the order over to Lydia," she said, handing him the menu.

"What are you having?" he asked.

Abbey pointed to her favourite pasta.

Sirius nodded. "I'll have the same," he said, handing her back the menu.

"And a drink?" she asked.

"Water, please," he said.

Abbey told Lydia their choices, ordering the two pasta dishes, water, and orange juice for herself.

100

"How are you?" he asked.

"I'm okay, but Jeff's attack straight after Jimmy's is frightening," she said.

"I have been thinking about what we might do to try to find out if Bill or Sarah are hiding something."

"What have you come up with?" Abbey asked.

"I will consult with Lily; she is a witch, you know?" he asked.

"Yes, I gathered," Abbey replied.

"She may have some magic that can help," he said.

"Can't you do it? Aren't you a wizard?" Abbey said.

Sirius laughed. "I forget you are new to this world. Wizards' magic is different. It works in the physical world. I am hoping Lily might have a potion that will reveal secrets.

"That would be fantastic," she said, and then her face fell. "But how would we get them to take it?"

"That's the next problem. Let's start with seeing what Lily can make up."

"Okay," she agreed.

"It is always possible that Jimmy was just taken by surprise," Sirius said.

"I would believe that if he had been hit on the back of the head," Abbey replied, "but he was bitten from the front, at his stomach."

Sirius agreed. It didn't seem to be a realistic explanation.

Lydia arrived with the food, and they ate for a while in companionable silence.

"The pasta is delicious," Sirius remarked.

Abbey smiled and told him it was her favourite dish. She looked at the clock, and it was nearly three. She took the last sip of her orange juice, having already finished her pasta. It was time to get the food ready for the early evening crowd. Sirius left, agreeing that he would call Lily straight away and he would let her know if Lily could help.

Abbey was at a dead end again, Sirius had messaged her before she had finished work to say that Lily had a recipe for a potion that would encourage truth, but it couldn't completely control the person to reveal everything. It would take a few days to brew, but she had agreed to start at once. All they could do was wait and hope that they could get Bill and Sarah to take the concoction. And it would either confirm their innocence or expose something that would give them a clue of where to go next. She would just have to wait. While she waited, she intended to use the time to read the books on magic that Lydia had brought in for her.

That evening, Abbey laid the books out on her coffee table, trying to decide which one to start with.

The first book was called simply "Thaumaturgy." Abbey had no idea what that even meant, but after skimming through the book, she thought it might mean the working of magic or something like that. She shrugged and placed it to one side.

The second book was titled, "Sorcery of Divination." Abbey shook her head and looked at the third book, which was named "Ensorceler Enchantments."

Abbey didn't know what that meant either, but she decided to give it a try. It was not like she was trying to perform magic. She only wanted to have some understanding of Sirius and the wizards who lived in this place. And she hoped it might confirm what Sirius had said he had been doing in the bar. But she thought it unlikely she would be so lucky to come across the explanation with this little bit of study.

She read until her eyes were red and her belly was rumbling. It was time for bed, and she hadn't eaten anything since lunch. She closed the book, not sure what, if anything, she had learnt.

Chapter 14

Abbey woke the next morning to knocking at her door. She pulled on her robe and slippers and went to answer the door. Bill stood on her doorstep. His face was haggard. He looked like he had aged twenty years. He asked if he could come in, and she directed him to the living room.

"You better call Sirius to join us," he said before she could excuse herself to get dressed.

She nodded and went to her bedroom. She dialled Sirius. She told him that Bill was at her home, and he had asked for him to join them. Sirius agreed he would be there in ten minutes. Abbey used the time to get dressed and brush her hair. She went directly to the kitchen, made a pot of coffee, and brought it into the living room with three cups. She poured Bill a cup, and he took a gulp and set the cup down. There was a loud knock at the door, and without saying anything to Bill, she went to answer it.

Abbey opened the door and waved Sirius in without speaking. She guided Sirius to the living room. He took a seat across from Bill, and Abbey sat down beside him. Abbey looked at Bill. He picked up the cup and took another swig of coffee.

Bill cleared his throat and then, in a voice that was almost a whisper, said, "I killed Jimmy."

Abbey gasped. She had known it was serious and had believed he would tell them something that would be a big clue to the murderer, but she had not expected this. Sirius and

104

herself had speculated that it might have been Bill or Sarah. But she recognized now that she hadn't really suspected Bill.

"Why did you kill him?" Sirius asked.

Bill looked straight at Sirius at this question. "I never intended to murder him," he said. "I had been drinking. I hardly remember what happened or what I was thinking. I was in a rage, the alcohol," he said, then shook his head. "He said something about me hiding and being afraid. You don't know me very well, but I have always had a temper. I had hoped that coming here to this haven would help me to control it. I hoped that staying away from the clan and living a quiet life would be enough to keep my temper in check. And it did for a time. Then I relaxed, and I started drinking, heavily drinking." He shook his head again. "There is no excuse," he said. "Jimmy was nothing but a friend to me. I can never forgive myself for what I have done…" he trailed off into silence.

Abbey didn't know what to say or what to think. This wasn't the mystery she had wanted to solve. This was just a sad story.

"Where did you commit the murder?" Sirius asked, his voice emotionless.

Abbey didn't know why he was still asking questions. Bill had admitted he killed him, that was the end.

"On the beach, in Misty Vale," Bill replied.

"Then why was his body in Ballybunion?" Abbey asked. It didn't make sense that his body was outside Misty Vale if he had killed him here.

"I panicked," Bill replied, his eyes turning to the floor. "When I came back to myself and realised what I had done, I couldn't stomach Sarah knowing. I carried the body to the cliffs at Ballybunion and threw him off. I hoped the sea would take him, and when he didn't return, people would believe he had just decided to leave Misty Vale." He fell silent again.

No one spoke for a little while. Abbey stayed quiet, letting the news sink in. Then she reached for her coffee cup and took a sip.

"I heard what you said the other night," Bill whispered.

Sirius looked towards the sky and shook his head slowly. "About being barred from Misty Vale?" he asked.

"Yes, if that is the consequence, then I am ready to accept it," Bill replied.

"You know that I have the magic to make it happen?" he asked.

Bill nodded.

"You won't only be barred from Misty Vale," Sirius told him. "You will be unwelcome in every other haven created by the same magic?" he stated.

Bill nodded again.

Abbey wanted to go to Bill and comfort him; he had taken a life, and some part of her felt he should be punished, but another part of her thought it was all just a tragic mistake. His remorse seemed all-consuming.

"It will take me a few days," Sirius said, "to prepare the magic. I suggest that we three keep this confession to ourselves until such time as I am ready to perform the ritual."

Bill looked up, his eyes filled with gratitude. He looked to Abbey to see if she agreed.

Abbey nodded.

"I suggest you take the time to ready yourself for departure," Sirius said.

Bill dipped his head in agreement.

"I will expect you to tell Sarah before you leave," Sirius informed him.

"I will," Bill said.

"Okay," Sirius approved.

Bill got up from his seat.

"What about Jeff?" Abbey asked.

"Jeff," Bill said, his face blank for a moment as though he couldn't place the name.

"No," he said. "I didn't have anything to do with Jeff's attack," he told them.

"Okay," Sirius said.

With a small bow of his head towards Abbey, Bill left.

Abbey placed her hands over her eyes and shook her head, sighing deeply.

Sirius remained silent for a couple of minutes. Then he spoke in a soft voice, "Do you belief him?" he asked.

"About Jeff?" Abbey said.

"No, about Jimmy," he clarified.

Abbey dropped her hands from her face, her eyes wide in shock. "Yes, I mean, why would he lie?" she asked.

"Why indeed," he said.

"You think he is covering for someone else?" she asked.

"Hmm," he said, "there is only one person whom I believe he would care sufficiently for to confess to murder."

"Sarah?" she asked.

"Indeed, Sarah," he replied.

"So, either his story is true, or he knows that Sarah murdered Jimmy, and he is shielding her from suspicion by confessing?" she asked.

"The only problem with him covering for her now is what has changed since yesterday? Why confess now?" Sirius asked.

"Maybe she told him she had murdered Jimmy last night?" she suggested.

"Perhaps," he agreed.

Abbey suddenly remembered what had changed since yesterday. "At the burial, I gave him a copy of the autopsy report," Abbey admitted.

Sirius raised his eyebrows at this. "That is interesting," he said. "Either he knew that the report pointed to him and therefore decided it was better to confess than wait to be discovered. Or it could be that he saw that the report pinpointed Sarah, and so he confessed to protect her."

"So, how will we know which one it is?" Abbey asked.

108

"I suggest we observe Sarah to see if there is any change in her demeanour. I also think we should meet again with Kane and ask him to look at the autopsy to see if there is anything which a wolf would notice about the details of the attack that is not obvious to us."

Abbey nodded. "So what should be done first?" she asked.

"I will leave you alone for now. Let you finish your morning routine," he said.

Abbey nodded gratefully. She really wanted to have a shower. She was a little shaken by Bill's confession and needed some time to pull herself together.

"I will contact Kane to see when he is free to meet with us," Sirius suggested. "I will contact you when I have agreed a time," he said.

Abbey saw him out and closed the door behind him. Laying her head on the inside of the door, she wanted it not to be true. She didn't want Bill to have been the murderer, not with such a tragic tale. But she did not think it being Sarah would make her any happier. She had not known Bill or Sarah until Jimmy's murder, but she had become fond of them in their short acquaintance.

Late that afternoon, Abbey knocked on Kane's door. Kane opened it almost immediately. He waved Abbey and Sirius in. "You are here about Jeff's attack?" he asked.

"No," Sirius said. "I'm sure Bill told you that Lily is caring for him?"

Kane nodded.

"We have no information other than what Bill told me when he found Jeff," Sirius told him. "I assume that he told you the same details when he visited you?" Sirius asked.

Kane nodded. "I suppose it was the same information. So Jeff is still in stasis?" he asked.

"Yes," Sirius confirmed, "his injuries were very severe, and I believe it is best for him to remain in stasis until Lily confirms he is sufficiently recovered to no longer be in danger."

Kane nodded in understanding.

Sirius reached into his jacket and pulled out the autopsy report. "We were hoping that you would be able to advise us," he said, passing the report over. "Dr Andrews carried out an autopsy on Jimmy," he said. "We wondered if there might be some aspect of the attack, which might provide a clue to a wolf, which would not be obvious to others," Sirius explained.

Kane pointed them to seats and took a seat himself behind his desk. He laid the report out on the table and started to read. Abbey sat quietly beside Sirius, giving Kane time to take in the details of the autopsy. He murmured and muttered to himself. As he read, he gasped at one point and stopped reading. He raised his eyes to Abbey and Sirius but didn't speak. He turned to the last page and sighed. When he had finished reading, he put the last page down on the table.

"Yes, it is thought-provoking," he said, shaking his head. "Why did he not change?" he asked.

"That is one of the questions," Abbey said.

"And what are the other questions?" he asked.

Abbey turned to Sirius, and he nodded. Abbey continued, "Is there anything about the physical attack which might provide clues as to the physical traits of the attacker?"

Kane nodded "yes." He said, "The wolf who killed Jimmy would have been a small, young, slight-built wolf."

Abbey didn't react. She kept her expression clear. "How can you tell?" she asked.

"The wound is at his stomach. Wolves normally attack at the neck," he said, placing his hand on his own neck. "Only a small, slight wolf would go for the middle," he explained. "The report also says that he did not change." He sighed deeply. "This would seem to indicate that he tried to reason with his attacker. This means that it was a friend who attacked him." He stopped talking and placed one hand up to his eyes.

Abbey looked at Sirius. She could see the same realisation that she had reached reflected in his eyes. But why? And how could Sarah behave so normally? How could she have appeared so shocked and heartbroken when they had told her Jimmy was dead! How could she have kept up such pretence even during the wake and burial? Something must be missing from her if she could murder the male who had provided protection to her and be able to keep up the act of grief!

Abbey didn't have any other questions for Kane. She could see he had come to the same

111

conclusion they had. That Sarah had murdered Jimmy.

Sirius stood up, and Kane gave him back the autopsy report. He waited for Abbey to join him.

"Do you think the same person who killed Jimmy also attacked Jeff?" Kane asked them.

"From what Bill told me, the two attacks seem very different," Sirius said. "So it seems unlikely."

Kane nodded.

They walked to Sirius's car. When he had offered to collect her earlier, Abbey had almost refused. But even if she had walked to Kane's house, with the revelation of the afternoon, she was happy for the lift home.

"Does this mean Sarah will be ejected from Misty Vale?" she asked in a small voice.

Sirius shook his head. "It will depend on the circumstances of the murder. It looks bad for her that Jimmy was in human form," he said.

"Because if it had been a fight and she was defending herself, he would have been in wolf form, too?" Abbey asked.

"Yes," he replied.

"Sarah, in human form, would be much less able to defend herself against Jimmy," she stated. "It could be that she had to change into her wolf in order to protect herself?" Abbey suggested.

This explanation gave her some comfort. If Jimmy had tried to attack Sarah, she would have been forced to protect herself the only way she could. But it still left Abbey unsatisfied because if she was only defending herself, why pretend grief. Why dump his body. She could have told Bill or anyone that Jimmy had attacked her. Sarah was a young woman, and everyone would have been sympathetic to her.

"Yes," Sirius agreed, "that could be a possible explanation."

"Maybe, she told Bill, and that's why he confessed?" Abbey proposed.

"It's possible," Sirius agreed, "but I think it more likely that he knew from reading the report."

"Sarah had problems with Jeff. Do you think she got desperate now that Jimmy is gone? Do you think she might have tried to get rid of Jeff now that she has no one to protect her?" Abbey asked. She didn't like what this thought indicated about Sarah. She didn't like that it seemed the young woman was devoid of human emotion. If she not only killed one person but then tried to murder a second one!

"No, I meant what I said to Kane. The differences in the two attacks make it unlikely that they were both performed by the same person," Sirius said.

"So, what do we do now?" Abbey asked.

"Bill has confessed. I am loathe to accuse Sarah until we find out the circumstances of the murder. I will delay my preparations for the expulsion. That will give Lily time to complete her potion. Then we will have to figure out a way to get Bill and Sarah to take it," Sirius suggested.

113

Abbey bobbed her head in agreement. She hoped that there was some justification, which would explain the murder. She also hoped that when Jeff was out of his stasis, he would not point to Sarah as his attacker.

Chapter 15

Abbey woke in the morning to knocking at her door. Surely Bill wasn't at her door again! She pulled on her robe and slippers and went to answer the door. Sarah stood on her doorstep; tears were streaming down her face. Abbey reached an arm around her back and drew her inside.

She sat down beside the younger woman on the couch. She didn't ask any questions, just waited for Sarah's tears to ease.

"I killed him," Sarah said.

Abbey hardly understood her through the sobs. She didn't know what to say to this. But she was relieved. She had known since yesterday that Sarah had taken Jimmy's life. Abbey had been through an emotional rollercoaster since she had found Jimmy's body. She had thought that nothing could affect her as much as discovering him that way.

But when Kane had confirmed yesterday that Sarah was the killer, even if he had not said so in words, Abbey had felt so disturbed by Sarah's behaviour; it had almost been worse. She only felt relief now that Sarah had confessed. Not only that she had confessed, but that she was showing sorrow for what she had done.

But then Abbey felt something was really wrong with this abrupt change in Sarah's behaviour. It didn't seem like she had been lying about killing Jimmy. It seemed like she had only found out that she had killed him. Could it be that

115

she had blanked it out and had only now remembered what she had done!

"I saw the autopsy report," Sarah mumbled between her tears. "It is exactly the same as my nightmares," she said.

"That doesn't mean—" Abbey started to say but stopped before the denial left her lips.

"It's more than that," Sarah continued. "The details of the attack," she said. "I'm the only wolf in Misty Vale who could have done it." Only whimpers escaped as Sarah dropped her head to her hands.

"But you don't remember killing him?" Abbey asked softly.

Sarah lifted her eyes to Abbey. "No, I don't remember," she whispered.

"I think we need to get you to remember," Abbey said. "That is the only way you can know for sure what happened. There might have been something else going on," Abbey said. Now that the other woman was showing emotion, Abbey wanted to believe that she was the victim. She wanted it to be that killing Jimmy was Sarah's only choice.

"Jimmy would never hurt me," Sarah said. It was the first time her voice had been clear since she had arrived at Abbey's door.

"Is there any reason you can think of why you would have attacked Jimmy?" Abbey asked.

Sarah shook her head.

"Then I think it is clear," Abbey said. "We need to get you to remember."

Sarah nodded. Her face was sombre, and the tracks of her tears were still visible.

Abbey went to her bedroom and got her phone. Coming back into the living room, she dialled Sirius's number.

Sirius answered.

"Sarah is here," Abbey said.

"I'm on my way," he answered.

Abbey went and got Sarah a glass of water and a box of tissues. She excused herself to get dressed. She dressed quickly. Then went to the hallway and opened the front door. Leaving it open, she went back to join Sarah. She was sitting subdued exactly as Abbey had left her. She had not drunk the water or dried the tear stains from her face. Abbey sat down beside her and put an arm around her shoulders. The other woman relaxed into her, and Abbey was glad to give her what little comfort she could.

Sirius poked his head into the living room and gestured behind him. He came into the room, and Bill followed him.

Sarah jumped up from the couch and threw herself at Bill. Bill caught her and wrapped her in a bear hug. Abbey could hear Sarah mumbling into Bill's shoulder that she was sorry. Abbey got up from the couch and indicated for Bill to sit down. He brought Sarah over and sat down beside her.

Abbey looked at Sirius. "We seem to have a bit of a conundrum," she said.

"I did it," Sarah said in a quiet voice.

117

"No," Bill said, "don't listen to her. She is trying to protect me."

"We already know you didn't kill him, Bill," Sirius told him. "We showed the autopsy report to Kane yesterday, and he explained the details of the report were inconsistent with an attack by a wolf of your size."

Bill's shoulders slumped. He turned his eyes to Sarah. "It will be okay, honey," he said in a fatherly tone.

"It won't be okay," she replied. "I killed Jimmy," she said. "I did a terrible thing. I murdered my friend," she told Bill. "There is no way it can ever be okay again. I will be ejected from Misty Vale forever," she stuttered. "It is the least I deserve for what I have done. But where can I even go? If I could kill a friend, I am too dangerous to be around anyone," Sarah told him, her words punctuated by her sobs.

"I will go with you," Bill said. "You won't be alone."

"Why don't we start with why you killed Jimmy?" Sirius asked.

"I don't know," Sarah wailed. "I can't remember."

Sirius's eyebrows raised at this. "Then how do you know it was you?" he asked.

"I read the autopsy, and I have been having nightmares. The details of the attack are exactly the same as my nightmares," Sarah said.

"And if we could restore your memories?" he asked.

"Yes, I need you to do that because I don't know why I would have killed him." Sarah stumbled over the word 'killed.' "I don't believe there is any reason I would want to."

"I cannot bring back your memory of that night, but I believe that Lily would be able to," Sirius replied. "Do you want me to contact her?"

"Yes," Sarah agreed. "I need to know why I, why I attacked him," Sarah stammered.

"And you, Bill?" Abbey asked. "You also confessed. Will you take a potion from Lily?"

Bill shrugged. "I don't have any memory problem, but whatever you need."

Sirius went outside. Returning a couple of minutes later. "Lily is on her way," he said.

Abbey went to the kitchen, and Sirius came with her. She pulled some eggs and vegetables from the fridge and started chopping them. She felt that today would not be easy, no matter what Sarah's memories revealed. Something tragic had happened. This was not some thrilling mystery. Abbey felt the same as she had when she had thought it had been Bill.

Something terrible had occurred, and Sarah had killed someone she had cared for. Sirius asked where the plates were, and she pointed him to the cupboard, pulling open a draw to where she kept the cutlery for him to dispense. She made two large omelettes and set them out on the kitchen table. She made some tea and coffee and brought them over to the table, asking Sirius to call Bill and Sarah to come and eat.

119

Abbey saw Sarah take a bite of omelette, and she was glad to see her eating. She looked so bad that Abbey wanted to take care of her. She sat down beside Sirius, taking a piece of the omelette for herself and pouring herself a cup of coffee. She had only just finished her piece of omelette when she heard the knock at the door. She got up to let Lily in.

Chapter 16

Lily arrived with a large bag and started taking ingredients from it. Placing them on the kitchen counter. "Right," Lily said. "What we have here," she said, indicating a small bottle of liquid, is a potion which will reveal secrets. "I suggest that Bill take this potion."

Bill did not look thrilled at this prospect.

"The potion will not reveal all your secrets," Lily reassured. "It will only reveal secrets in relation to matters on which we question you."

"We will keep our questions to areas relating to Jimmy's death," Sirius confirmed.

Bill nodded and held out his hand. Before he could take it, she continued, "For Sarah," she said, looking to the young woman, "I will have to cook up something," pointing to the ingredients. "This should restore your lost memories."

"Thank you," Sarah said in a quiet voice.

Sirius stood up and cleared off the kitchen table, leaving only the tea and coffee.

"You may as well take it now while I prepare the potion for Sarah," Lily told Bill.

Bill uncorked the bottle and drank it down in one gulp.

"How long will it be before it takes effect?" Abbey asked.

"Almost immediately," Lily answered, "like magic!" she said.

121

Abbey gave a small smile at this response, even though she felt there was little to smile about.

"Why don't you start?" Sirius suggested to Abbey.

Abbey looked directly at Bill and asked, "Why did you confess to murdering Jimmy?"

Bill answered straight away, "To protect Sarah."

Sarah grabbed Bill's hand, and Abbey could see that the other woman had already figured this out. She continued, "Why did you think that confessing would protect Sarah?"

Bill looked at Sarah, his eyes shadowed with sorrow. "I read the report, and I knew that only Sarah could have killed him because of the nature of the injury. I also knew that the only reason Jimmy wouldn't have changed form is if Sarah or a child had attacked him."

"So, if you believed Sarah had murdered your friend, why would you confess in her place?" Abbey asked.

Looking at her, he said, "Jimmy must not have been the male I believed him to be. The only reason I can think of for Sarah to kill him is if it was in self-defence."

"No," Sarah said.

He looked at her. "You must have blocked out the memory because of the trauma of someone you had trusted so much attacking you."

Sarah shook her head. "I can't believe that Jimmy would have attacked me. He has always been nothing but kind and protective towards me."

122

Tears gathered in her eyes as she spoke, but she wiped them away.

"Can you think of any other questions?" she asked Sirius.

"Why do you think she dumped his body outside of Misty Vale?" he asked the other man.

"I thought she had probably panicked when she realised what she had done."

Lily had continued to brew the potion for Sarah while Bill had answered these questions.

"Do you know anything about Jeff's attack?" Abbey asked. Knowing that this was diverging from the agreed secrets they would ask about, but felt she had to ask.

"No," Bill replied.

"Do you have any questions, Lily?" Abbey asked.

"No, I think that about covers it," she replied.

"I'm sorry, Sarah," Bill said.

"You have no reason to be sorry. I'm sorry about how I reacted when you told me you had murdered Jimmy. I should have known that you would not have attacked him. Instead, I asked you to leave. It was just that when you told me you had killed him, it was like I had lost you as well as him," Sarah said.

Bill hugged her.

"The second potion is ready," Lily said, pouring some of the liquid into a cup for Sarah. She handed her the cup, and Sarah drank it down.

"What do I do now?" asked Sarah.

"Give it a minute. It is a complex process. You will either start to feel a slight ruffling in your brain or—"

Before Lily could complete the sentence, Sarah cried out in pain and placed both her hands on her head. Bill dropped to his knees in front of her and took both her hands.

"Are you okay?" he asked.

"Or," Lily continued, "you will get a strong pain in your head. It shouldn't last long," the older woman reassured.

Sarah dropped her hands from her face. It was pain-free, but her complexion had turned ashen. "I remember," she said.

"It was after closing. It had been a quiet night, so we had closed early. I was in the kitchen finishing the cleaning. It was nearly midnight. I walked to the back of the kitchen, and with some chalk I had in my pocket, I drew marks on the floor and a bright light shone from where I had drawn the marking. Jimmy came into the kitchen just as I finished. I changed form on seeing him and started to attack him. He was talking the entire time, trying to get me to calm down and change back." Sarah halted for a second, tears streaming down her face. "He never even started to change," she said. "He didn't want to hurt me. He didn't even try to defend himself," she said, her words ending in gulping cries.

Bill had still been holding her hands, but he dropped them to pull her forward into another hug. Abbey grabbed some tissues and handed them to her. Sirius stood like a statue, his face

124

blank of any emotion. Lily merely appeared to be interested in hearing the story.

"I didn't change back," Sarah cried. "I became even more feral in my attack. I ribbed out his stomach," she said, "and his body fell directly at the light in the ground." The last word came out in a wail, and she broke down into inconsolable sobs, with Bill holding her tightly in comfort.

When her tears had eased a little, Sirius asked, "How did you know how to make the marks to open the portal?"

Sarah looked up at him, her eyes wide in confusion. "I don't—"

Abbey knew she had been about to say, I don't know, but instead, Sarah continued.

"I had forgotten," she said. "I had gone to Ballybunion the day before to get some ingredients for the dish I wanted to cook that evening. Just before I stepped through the mist to come home, a tall male approached me," she said. "He placed his hands on my head." She raised both her hands to her temple. "And then I stepped into Misty Vale and completely forgot having met him." She turned her eyes to Sirius.

Abbey could see by Sirius's face, both serious and filled with concern, that this meant something to him.

"What do you remember about how he looked?" Sirius asked.

"He was tall, but that is all I can tell you. He was covered in a long cloak-like coat with a hood, which covered his head," Sarah said, raising her hands upwards.

Sirius looked at Abbey and asked finally, "Do you know anything about Jeff's attack?"

"No," Sarah replied.

"Thank you, Sarah," he said. "There is much to think about. Please, don't have any further worries about your place here," he said softly.

But Abbey could hear the tension in his voice and see it in his bearing.

"I think it best that Bill takes you home now," he said.

Bill nodded; his face relaxed for the first time since he had arrived at Abbey's house that morning. Sirius's words had taken away his worries. But Abbey could see that what Sarah had revealed had made Sirius more concerned rather than less.

"But what happened to me?" Sarah asked.

"It sounds like you were the subject of a compulsion," Sirius told her. "Please do not blame yourself any longer for Jimmy's death. You were not the killer; you were merely the instrument of the murderer," he said.

Abbey was glad that she had read that book that Lydia had given her. She had thought she hadn't learnt anything from reading it. But Abbey at least knew what Sirius meant when he said Sarah had been under a compulsion. The book explained it as a strong spell that took over the will of the subject to compel them to perform a specific task or tasks. It said that once the compulsion had been fulfilled, the subject would be released from the enchantment.

126

Abbey saw from Sarah's face that she didn't know whether this relieved her of blame or not, but she nodded and allowed Bill to lead her from the room. "So, if she was the subject of compulsion, who is the real murderer?" Abbey asked Sirius.

"A very powerful wizard," Sirius said. "Unfortunately, I do not know who the wizard is. But he is not a resident of Misty Vale. I am the only wizard in Misty Vale who is powerful enough to have placed Sarah under such a powerful compulsion."

Abbey was glad that Sirius had said these words. For if, a couple of days earlier, she had discovered the murder had been by someone under a compulsion. And someone else had told her that only Sirius would be powerful enough to perform it. Abbey would have thought him to be the murderer.

"I began to suspect that the murder of Jimmy might not be so straightforward last night. Bill arrived at my door looking for a place to stay. He told me that he had confessed to Sarah that he had murdered Jimmy. He said that she had been frightened of him and asked him to leave. He has no other home in Misty Vale, so he came to me."

Abbey nodded; she had been surprised when Sirius had arrived with Bill in tow. But Sarah believing Bill that he had murdered Jimmy was consistent with her not remembering attacking him. "So that thing," Abbey said, placing her hands at her temples in the way Sarah had indicated. "That was the wizard placing the compulsion on Sarah?" she asked.

"Yes, it is how a compulsion is performed, and it would take a very powerful wizard to create such a strong urge," he confirmed.

And then another idea came to her. "You think Jeff was trying to get to the source as well?" she asked.

"Yes," he replied. "I think he was trying to get to the source."

"You have an idea about who attacked him?" Abbey asked.

"Yes, I think whoever placed the compulsion on Sarah attacked Jeff. I think they gravely wounded him outside of Misty Vale and, under compulsion, sent him back into the haven. He was meant to make his way to the source and die there the same way Jimmy had. But they miscalculated, Jeff's wounds were too severe, and he didn't make it."

"But you know something else, as well," Abbey said. She could see he was debating what to tell her. She saw the moment he decided to speak. Lily saw it, too, and sat down at the table. Abbey sat as well.

Chapter 17

"There was a murder in Misty Vale ten years ago," Sirius began.

Abbey remained silent, but she recognised the beginning of the story that Tobias had told her.

"The owner of the bar, Paul Kelly, he was also a werewolf. When I recognised Jimmy on the beach that day, I suspected that the two murders were connected. But Lily's," he said, indicating the other woman, "autopsy reassured me that they were not connected. Paul was murdered by a vampire."

"Are you sure it was a vampire?" Abbey asked.

"Yes," Lily answered. "I carried out the examination on the body at Sirius's request."

"I visited Tobias the other day, and he told me about Paul's murder," Abbey admitted.

"You visited Tobias," Sirius said. He did not seem to be pleased with this news.

"Yes," Abbey replied.

"Why did you visit him?" Sirius asked, his eyes hooded.

Lily put her hands up to her mouth and stifled a laugh.

"I was suspicious of you after I saw you coming out of the bar," she said. Abbey shook her head. "Why do you now think they are connected."

"There is a similarity that needs further investigation," Sirius informed her. "The vampire, Simon, claimed to have blacked out; this would

129

not be normal for vampires, but Simon was very young. I accepted the explanation, but he had proven to be dangerous, and therefore, he was ejected from Misty Vale."

"But the vampire, could he have placed a compulsion on Sarah?" Abbey asked.

"No," Sirius replied, "that is not within the abilities of vampires. But he may have been a victim of the wizard who placed the compulsion on Sarah." Sirius sighed deeply. He looked directly into Abbey's eyes. "If the two murders are connected, it is very serious for Misty Vale."

"Why would someone want to target the owners of the bar?" Abbey asked.

"You said you saw the well in the kitchen of the bar when I was there?" he asked.

"Yes," Abbey agreed.

"I am telling you this, but if you reveal this information to anyone else, I will banish you from Misty Vale forever and remove all your memories of this place," he told her.

Abbey nodded in understanding that what he was telling her was a great secret.

"Misty Vale is built on a natural well of magic. That is what makes this place possible. The well in the bar is the source of that magic. Misty Vale selects the owner of the bar as the protector of the source. Jimmy was the protector; Paul was the previous protector. I had also long believed that Sarah would be the next protector. By having Sarah kill Jimmy and her be banished from Misty Vale, two protectors would be removed in one step."

130

Abbey gasped. "And if there is no protector?" she asked.

"That would make it easier for anyone who wished to bring Misty Vale down. This would be necessary if one wished to access the source. The source is a great spring of power. Which would be tempting to a wizard," Sirius told her.

"So, you believe that a wizard is trying to get to the source?" Abbey asked.

"Yes," Sirius replied, "and in order to find out who that wizard is, I intend to draw Simon back to Misty Vale," he said. Then, turning to Lily, he asked, "If I bring Simon here, would you be able to bring back his memories from so long ago?"

"It will take a more complex recipe, but yes, I believe I will be able to restore any memories he has lost," Lily confirmed.

"Okay, I will work on drawing him back," Sirius said.

Abbey smiled; the murder was turning out to be a lot more complicated than she had originally supposed. But she was relieved that Sarah had not been responsible for Jimmy's death. "How long will it take for Simon to return?" Abbey asked.

"We don't know how far away he is from here; it may take some time for him to arrive," he said.

Abbey nodded. "Okay, so we wait for him to arrive, and then Lily gives him the potion, and we find out if the two murders are really

131

connected. But what do we do in the meantime?" Abbey asked. "One protector of the source has been murdered. Sarah must also be in danger. But if Jeff, who has no connection to the bar, was also injured to such an extent that it took the magic of both Lily and you to save him, is anyone safe? Or is it only the werewolves who are in danger?" Abbey asked.

"Once Simon arrives to confirm that this is an attack on Misty Vale and not only an attack on the werewolves, I will close the border. No one in or out of Misty Vale bar anyone from leaving, and anyone who is outside will not be able to reenter until the danger has passed."

Chapter 18

Abbey was in a state of nervous anticipation. She spent the next day working in the diner, but it was not enough to distract her from waiting for the vampire, Simon, to arrive. It wasn't until the second day working in the diner that she saw Sirius walking towards the diner.

Putting his head in the door. "Simon is approaching the border," he told Abbey.

Abbey turned to Lydia. "Go," Lydia said.

Abbey thanked her, pulling off her apron and going outside.

Abbey stood beside Sirius at the beach in Misty Vale. She waited and saw a slim male of average height come through the mist and fall to his knees on the sand. He looked up and saw Sirius. Being a vampire, he was already pale, but his eyes and mouth opened wide in a rictus of horror.

"I did not want to come here," he said. "Something drew me here, please you have to believe me?" he begged.

"I know," Sirius reassured him. "It was I who called you here."

The vampire's face relaxed, and he looked at Sirius. "Why?" he asked.

"The owner of the bar has been murdered," Sirius said.

The vampire's eyes filled with fear again.

"You are not under suspicion for the second murder. The two murders have certain

133

similarities which raised questions about the death of Paul Kelly," Sirius explained.

The vampire got to his feet. "You mean," he said, but then he stopped and shook his head. "I'm sorry, but I know I killed Paul."

"I know that you killed him, but there is a possibility that there were extenuating circumstances," Sirius said. "I am not promising anything, and you will have to take a potion made by Dr Lily Andrews," he explained.

"If there is any chance, I am willing to do whatever it takes," the vampire replied.

"You will not move freely around Misty Vale," Sirius instructed. "You will stay in my home, and you will not leave there without my permission. Should you not follow these instructions, I will kill you," Sirius promised.

The vampire agreed.

"I will let you know when the potion is ready," he told Abbey.

Abbey nodded and left them to go back to work. Back to waiting for the next step.

Abbey was not working that day and was glad of that when Sirius called to invite her to his home. "Lily has completed the potion for Simon, and she is on her way here," he said. "She told me that we need you to be present," he told her.

Abbey could hear in his voice that he was unsure if it was a good idea for her to be present. But she was glad that Lily had insisted. She had been involved in the investigation since the beginning. Lily was right that she should be there for Simon's questions. She took the directions

134

from Sirius and arrived at his house fifteen minutes later. His house was a grand three-story country home with lots of windows and steps leading to the front door. She knocked. She was faintly surprised to see Sirius when he answered. The house was so grand, she had expected to see a butler.

Sirius led her into a large sitting room with three distinct seating areas of large couches and overstuffed armchairs. There was a fire burning brightly in the large fireplace in the centre of the room. Lily sat on an armchair with a coffee table in front of her. She was taking a syringe from her bag, and she put it on the table beside five or six other items already there. Lily looked over at Abbey as she arrived and said "hello" but continued with her work.

"Okay, if we are all ready, come sit here, young man," Lily said, tapping the chair beside her. Simon took the seat she had indicated. "You should also sit down, Abbey," she said, pointing to the seat at her other side. "Because you are a vampire, this potion will work a little differently," she explained. "I will need to inject the potion into your neck," she said.

The vampire nodded.

"Also, as you are a vampire, there will be one additional ingredient, and it also needs to be fresh," she said.

"What ingredient?" he asked.

Lily looked at Abbey. "Human blood," she said.

Abbey started shaking and felt all the blood leave her face. "You want my blood?" she asked Lily.

"No need to look so frightened. I will only need a very small amount," she explained. "No more than you would provide if you were having a blood test," Lily told her, pointing to a small vial on the table.

Abbey wasn't thrilled to be supplying her blood to a vampire. But she was glad that it would be injected into him and he wouldn't be drinking it. She was also relieved that it was only a small amount. She now knew why Lily had insisted she be there. She felt her ego deflate. It was not that she was some amazing investigator. She was merely an ingredient!

"Roll up your sleeve," Lily instructed her.

She rolled up her sleeve, and the other woman tapped a couple of times on one of her veins and then injected the syringe into her arm and drew a small amount of blood. She handed Abbey a small cotton ball, placed it over the wound, and placed Abbey's hand on top.

"Keep pressure on it for a couple of minutes," Lily told her. "Until the bleeding has stopped."

Lily took the blood-filled syringe and plunged the blood into a small bottle, which was already half filled with a green liquid. The resulting fluid was a mustard yellow. Lily selected a second syringe and drew the liquid from the bottle. "Pull down the neck of your shirt," she ordered the vampire. He did as commanded. Lily injected the liquid into a vein in his neck. The vampire winced as the syringe went in, but he relaxed once the procedure was completed.

"Now what?" the vampire asked. Grimacing, his eyes flashing red.

Abbey jumped up from her seat. Sirius, who had stood during the entire process, came over and placed a hand on her shoulder. "It is fine," he reassured her. "It is only a side effect of the potion working through his system." Abbey looked at him and gave him a slight smile, embarrassed by her overreaction. She sat down again and watched. A couple of minutes later, the vampire's eyes returned to their bright blue.

He looked up at Sirius. "I don't feel any different," he said.

Then, the vampire's eyes opened wide.

Chapter 19

Simon spoke, "I remember that I was in the bar. I was the last customer. Paul told me it was time to leave, but I hadn't finished my drink, a Bloody Mary," he said. "Paul told me to drink up. I wasn't happy, and Paul growled at me, and that was it. I attacked him," he said, turning his downcast eyes up to Sirius.

"There's more," he said. "He didn't have time to react. My attack was so unexpected. I ripped his throat out before he had time to defend himself or change into a wolf." His shoulders slumped. "I hoped there would be something that would be different from what I thought I had done," he said. But then his eyes opened wide, and he looked startled. "I don't know why I did this, but while he was bleeding to death, I dragged his body to the kitchen of the bar," he said. "I traced something on the ground with his blood, and a light or a hole in the ground appeared.

Abbey's mouth dropped open, and she could see the same surprise on Lily's face. Sirius's face was blank, and Abbey thought he had probably hoped that the two murders were not connected. If they were, what did that mean for Misty Vale?

Simon continued, "I let him die on that spot. When he was dead, I moved his body back to the bar and cleaned up the blood in the kitchen. When I returned to the bar, I came back to myself. That's when I went to Tobias." He shook his head, his eyes wide. He looked around at Lily and Abbey.

"What were you doing earlier that day?" Abbey asked. The details of Simon's story were so similar to Sarah's that Abbey had no doubt that Simon was also influenced by the same wizard.

Simon shrugged. "I had been in London for a few weeks, and I only arrived back at Misty Vale that morning." He frowned and then said, "I met someone before I entered." He shook his head. "I don't remember," he said.

"Retrace your steps from when you arrived in Ballybunion," Abbey suggested.

"I parked my car at the caravan park and walked down the hill to the beach. I took the steps down and walked towards the cliff. It was not quite sunrise, and the mist was starting to come in from the sea. I saw a man standing beside the cliff. He turned as I arrived. I didn't recognise him," Simon said, then he halted. "I said hi to him as I approached. He reached a hand to me, and I thought he was going to shake my hand, but instead, he reached for my head." His eyes wide, shaking his head, he continued, "He placed his hands on either side of my head." He indicated the same place on the temples that Sarah had. "I don't know why I didn't react." He shrugged.

"What did he do?" Simon asked Sirius.

"I think he placed you under a compulsion," Sirius told him.

The vampire's eyes cleared, and a tension that Abbey hadn't noticed seemed to lift from him. "Does this mean," he asked in a quiet voice, "that I am not to blame for Paul's murder?" His voice rose as he spoke.

"It would seem so," Sirius replied.

The vampire's face filled with a large smile that brightened up his whole face.

"Do you remember what he looked like?" Sirius asked.

"Yes," he said, and Sirius's shoulders relaxed.

"He was tall and slim, about six foot tall," he said. Raising a hand about five inches over his own head. "He had light-blond hair, and his eyes were green." He bobbed his head and looked to Sirius. "That's it."

Sirius nodded. "As much as I have enjoyed having you stay," he said, "I believe you will find Misty Vale will have assigned you a home."

The vampire stood immediately.

"Do you know where it is?" Sirius asked.

"Yes," he said, smiling and giving a small laugh.

He was so happy that Abbey couldn't help but smile, too. But once he had left, she made eye contact with Sirius, and her smile left her face. He was frowning, and he plopped down on a couch across from Abbey.

"I am happy for Simon," Lily said, verbalizing Abbey's thoughts, "but this is very bad for Misty Vale."

Sirius remained quiet for a few minutes; his eyes glazed. Then he looked up and, reaching into his pocket, he pulled out his phone. He passed the phone to Abbey. "Call Sarah and Bill to come here straight away."

Abbey took the phone, and she rang Bill's number. He answered quickly, "Sirius?" he said.

"No, it's Abbey," she replied. "There's been a development," she told him. "Please come to Sirius's house and bring Sarah, come immediately," she said. Bill agreed, and Abbey hung up, passing the phone back to Sirius.

"There is something else," Lily said. "Jeff has come out of his stasis, and although he is not ready to be moved, he was able to talk," Lily said.

Abbey's ears perked up at this news.

"He told me he was attacked by a wizard. He was held immobile while the wounds were inflicted. He also described how the wizard placed his hands on either side of his temple," Lily told them. "He said that is the last thing he remembers before waking up in my home this morning."

Before either of them could comment on this, Abbey heard a car pulling up to Sirius's house. She looked at him and went to let Bill and Sarah in. They both looked confused, but Abbey thought it best to let Sirius explain. Abbey led them to the sitting room. Sirius looked at Bill and Sarah but did not speak. Abbey sighed and began to talk.

"Are you aware of Paul Kelly?" Abbey asked. Thinking this was the best place to start.

Bill shook his head.

"Yes," Sarah said, "he was the owner of the bar before Jimmy. I met him when I was a child."

"Are you aware that he was murdered?" Abbey asked Sarah.

She frowned and then nodded. "I think I remember hearing that," she replied.

Abbey continued, "He was murdered by a vampire by the name of Simon. Some of the details you gave about Jimmy's death reminded Sirius of what Simon had told him after he had killed Paul. Sirius sent for him to return to Misty Vale. He arrived yesterday, and Lily gave him a potion today, which revealed that he had also been influenced by a wizard to commit the murder."

Sarah frowned. "But why two murders, ten years apart, of the owner of the bar? What could be so important about the bar that it would be worth murder?" Sarah asked.

Abbey looked at Sirius, her eyebrows raised. Surely, he didn't expect her to explain this part.

"The bar is important," Sirius spoke, much to Abbey's relief. "When your memories were restored, you told us about drawing symbols on the ground in the kitchen and a light in the ground," Sirius reminded her.

"Yes," Sarah confirmed.

"What you have not been aware of is that there is a well of magic under the bar, which is accessed from the point on which you drew the runes," he explained.

Bill did not react to this. Abbey thought that maybe he had understood something from Sarah's story the other day that she had not. Sarah's hands went up and covered her mouth.

"The well is the source of the magic which makes Misty Vale possible. I now believe that the reason for Jimmy's murder and indeed for the murder of Paul Kelly was to make the source vulnerable," Sirius said.

"The owner of the bar is also the protector of that source of magic," he told Sarah. "Jimmy's murder and his blood being spilt over the source created two vulnerabilities. One, it removed the protector and two, it weakened the magic by the use of his blood." Sarah was shaking now.

"I nearly exposed Misty Vale?" she asked, her eyes wide and fearful.

"You were used to try to expose Misty Vale," Abbey reminded her.

"There was also a third effect of Jimmy's murder," Sirius told her.

Sarah looked at him, her brow furrowed.

"You are to be the new owner of the bar," he told her.

"Me?" she said, looking at Bill.

"Yes, you will be the new owner, there is no doubt," Sirius confirmed. "As the new owner, you will also be the new protector of the source."

"But I am not strong," Sarah said, looking at Bill again.

"Being the protector is not about physical strength. It is about what is in your heart. In your heart, you would die to protect Misty Vale. The magic of Misty Vale recognizes that and has chosen you."

Sarah's shoulders raised at this, and she held her head up high. It was the first time Abbey had seen any strength in the younger woman. Abbey could see that Sirius was correct, and Sarah loved Misty Vale and would do anything to protect it.

"The wizard selected you to kill Jimmy for precisely that reason. I do not know how he knew you would be the next protector, but he did. By having you banished from Misty Vale, he would have removed two protectors in one step," Sirius said. Looking at Bill, he said, "There is no other possible protector in Misty Vale at this time. Bill, your willingness to leave Misty Vale, firstly to cover for Sarah and secondly to go with her, means that your loyalty is not to this place."

Bill nodded, and Sarah took his hand.

"The wizard has failed in having you banished, Sarah," Sirius told her. "He will not stop in his attempt to unravel the magic of Misty Vale."

Bill's shoulders squared, and Abbey could see he understood what Sirius was telling them.

"The logical next step for him is, therefore, to remove you," he told her.

"I won't go," Sarah said. "I won't leave Misty Vale again. I will stay here."

Sirius nodded, and he reached out and touched Sarah's hand. "If he cannot get you banished and you will not leave, then he will send someone to kill you."

Sarah flinched at the words. "I will not leave," she said, her voice strong.

"That is as I had expected," he told her. "We must, therefore, ensure that you are safe. To that end, I suggest that both Lily and I place enchantments upon you to assist in keeping you protected."

"Bill, I will also ask that you undergo a binding to protect Sarah for the rest of your life," Sirius asked.

"I will swear an oath to do so. There is no need to bind me," Bill said.

"I know you would willingly do so; the problem is not your free will," Sirius said. "Or actually, it is your free will. You would freely protect Sarah, but that would still leave you open to compulsion, and as the person closest to her, you will have the most opportunity to harm her. This would make you a likely target for the wizard. The binding will make it impossible for the wizard to place you under a compulsion."

"I will undergo the binding," Bill agreed.

Chapter 20

"Outside is best for me," Sirius suggested.

Abbey knew that she was not needed, but she didn't want to miss seeing Sirius perform his magic. So she moved to join the group going outside.

"I will leave you for now," Lily told the group. "I will have to work on the protection magic," she said, putting her hand up to her chin. "I think a protection charm will work best for Sarah," Lily said, walking to her car with her back to the group.

"You first, Sarah," Sirius called. She walked over to him. "You should kneel down," he said, and Sarah knelt. "You will feel a sensation of heat, but there should be no pain," he told her. Sirius crouched down beside her and placed one palm on the ground. He placed his other hand on the top of Sarah's head. He started mumbling words in a language Abbey didn't recognize. Abbey saw a light flowing from the ground up Sirius's arm and back down his other hand into Sarah's head and then flow all around her. Sarah glowed with the light for a few seconds, and then the light faded away.

"How do you feel?" Abbey asked.

Sarah shrugged. "Normal," she replied.

"As you should," Sirius told her.

"Bill, you are next," Sirius called to him. Sarah arose, and Bill went to take her place.

"No, you should remain standing," he told Bill. "I'm sorry to tell you that this will be unpleasant," he said with a wry smile.

Bill gave a sardonic smile back and stood beside him. Sirius again reached to the ground, staying stooped with his hands on the ground for a little while.

Light again drew up from the ground and into Sirius's body. Then he stood up, and with both his hands, he pushed the light into Bill's body. Bill shook and shuddered as the light filled him. He didn't look like he was in pain, but it seemed as if he was having a seizure. Once the light was surrounding Bill, Sirius began to mutter again in that strange language.

When he had finished, he asked Bill, "How are you?"

"I feel like a light bulb," Bill quipped.

Sirius smiled. "Yes, I have heard it described similarly before."

"Are you okay?" Sarah asked him.

Bill shook his entire body like a dog shaking off water. "Yes, I am," he reassured Sarah.

"Sarah, Lily will contact you directly when the charm is ready. Bill, if anything unusual happens, call me immediately, no matter the time, day, or night," Sirius told him, and Bill nodded.

Sarah gave Abbey a hug, and they both thanked Sirius and left.

"So, is that it?" Abbey asked.

"No, I will need to place an alarm on the border of Misty Vale. Should anyone come close without an invitation, it will alert me. Hopefully, that will be enough to stop the wizard from attempting to harm Sarah."

Abbey nodded. This sounded like a good idea.

"Come inside for a moment, Abbey. There are a couple of things that I think you should know," Sirius said, his voice serious.

Abbey walked ahead of him back inside.

"Abbey, we haven't known each other very long, but I think this situation has brought us together in a way that transcends time."

Abbey agreed. She had become close to Sirius and had learnt to trust him in the last few days.

"You are aware that I am very old?" he asked her.

"Yes, I had heard that," she said.

"What I am about to tell you is a secret. Only one other person in Misty Vale is aware of this secret," he told her.

"Tobias?" Abbey asked.

"Yes, Tobias."

"I am not a very old wizard," he told her. "I know that many in Misty Vale believe me to be over two hundred years old. The truth is, I am an ancient wizard."

Abbey gasped, her hands covering her mouth. "How ancient?" she asked.

"I am over one thousand years old," he told her.

Abbey sank back into the couch; she couldn't get her mind around such an age. "What must we be to you?" she asked.

Sirius gave her an ironic smile. "Yes," he said. "You comprehend the difficulties my great age causes. There comes a time when you lose touch with humanity. Where even the oldest vampire seems like a child in comparison. Most vampires do not choose to live long beyond the age of three hundred. And that is the age I would say that I too disconnected from humanity, in all its forms," he told her, indicating around him to the community of Misty Vale. "I felt it happen, and I felt a great darkness fill me," he said. His eyes glazing with a deep sadness, he looked to the floor.

He then looked directly at Abbey. "That is when I decided to create the first sanctuary of Misty Vale."

Abbey's eyes opened wide; she felt all the blood drain from her face. Sirius was the creator of Misty Vale!

"As wizards age, our magic grows, too. I felt the natural magic of this place call to me. I came here, to this deserted place. There was no Misty Vale at that time. Only the land on which Ballybunion now stands. But this place called to me. I stood on the cliff at Ballybunion, and I poured my magic into this land and with it, I created Misty Vale. I then stepped over the border and saw my home. I had not called on my magic to create a home for me. Misty Vale used my magic and provided me with what I needed most: a haven."

Abbey felt herself sympathize with Sirius, who had been so lost and alone. So far removed from the world that he only wanted to escape.

"It was many years before the next resident found this place. In truth, I cannot even tell you how long or who that first resident was. But over time, more and more came, and I continued to feed my magic into Misty Vale. Releasing my magic helped me to control the darkness, but I was still lost to humanity. I then found a solution," he said, looking at Abbey. "I not only placed my magic into Misty Vale, but I also discharged my memories, too," he said with a slight smile.

"As my memories left me, retaining only the memories which equalled that of a live span of one hundred years, I felt my humanity return."

Abbey smiled.

"You may wonder why I am choosing to tell you this?"

Abbey hadn't wondered, but of course, there must be a very important reason for Sirius to reveal such an enormous secret to her. "Yes," she replied.

"Misty Vale is in danger," he told her.

Abbey nodded; she already knew this.

"The only way for me to fight the wizard who seeks to unravel my magic is to restore my memories and drawback to me some portion of the magic I have given to Misty Vale."

"I can understand that," Abbey said.

"I will not be the man you know now when my memories are restored to me," he told her. "I will be dark, and I will be dangerous."

Abbey nodded. He needed to be dangerous if he was to defeat the threat to Misty Vale.

"I will not only be dangerous to the wizard Abbey. I will be dangerous to you."

Abbey gasped.

"I will be dangerous to anyone who gets in my way," he told her.

"But afterwards?" Abbey asked.

"I do not know," he said, shaking his head. "I do not know if I will again choose to release my memories. I do not know who or what I will be in the end."

Abbey sighed. "I understand," she said.

"Before morning, I will close the border and place the alarm, which will let me know should anyone try to gain entry to Misty Vale," he told her. "I will wait until Lily has given Sarah the charm to draw back my memories." He halted for a moment, taking Abbey's hand. "Thank you for understanding, Abbey. I hope that we will be friends again when this is over. I will be calling a meeting of Misty Vale this evening, telling everyone what has happened to Jimmy and Jeff. I will also be telling them that the entry to Misty Vale will be blocked."

Abbey nodded, understanding that this was the only way. She stood up, and he stood, too. Abbey reached up and placed a kiss on his cheek. Sirius wrapped his arms around her and hugged her for a moment, then he released her. Abbey stepped back, and without looking at him again, she left. Her bike waited outside, and her eyes filling with tears, she cycled home.

The call had gone out through Misty Vale, and Abbey stood at the beach. She stood beside Lydia and Rick. They had just closed up the diner. All around her stood all the inhabitants of Misty Vale, many of which she had never seen before. She noticed a large, strong-looking, grey-haired man. She wondered if this was the old wolf Sean Sirius had previously mentioned. She also saw Belinda standing beside Kane and some other males whom she recognised as members of the clan. She did not see Tobias, but she was sure he was there.

"I have called this meeting to tell you that Abbey," he said, indicating in her direction, "and I have been investigating Jimmy's murder and also Jeff's attack."

Abbey looked around for Sarah on hearing this, and she saw her holding onto Bill's arm. Sarah caught her eye and nodded, reassuring Abbey that she knew what Sirius was about to reveal.

"Misty Vale is in danger," he said.

Abbey could see many concerned faces at these words.

"All the peoples of Misty Vale are in danger," he told them. "There is a dark wizard who is trying to gain access to Misty Vale with the intention of disrupting the haven. In trying to do so, he ensorceled Sarah to make her kill Jimmy." He paused.

152

Abbey saw and heard mutterings of shock on Sirius's speaking Sarah's name. But no one questioned what Sirius had told them. No one believed that Sarah, the gentlest of werewolves, would have killed Jimmy unless she was under a spell.

Sirius continued, "I believe he also mortally wounded Jeff outside of Misty Vale and placed a compulsion on him to come back here to try to disrupt the magic," he said. He didn't explain how the murder of Jimmy or Jeff would have helped the wizard to threaten Misty Vale. At this time, everyone was too shocked by the revelations to question this.

"What this means is that anyone who leaves Misty Vale at this time is in danger of either being used as Sarah was or being murdered like Jimmy." He stopped talking again. The crowd murmured amongst themselves about what was to be done.

Sirius interrupted the chatter, "I intend to close the border to Misty Vale," he said. Most people looked pleased with this pronouncement. "What this means," he went on, "is that anyone who leaves Misty Vale now may not be able to regain entrance for some time to come," he said.

"So, we are prisoners here, that's what you are saying," said one middle-aged male, whom Abbey did not recognise.

"You are not prisoners," Sirius said. "You are free to leave."

"And why should you have the say as to whether the border gets closed," another young male said.

"I am the only wizard here who is strong enough to close the border. I am also strong enough to fight the wizard if he breaks through," Sirius informed them, with no arrogance or false modesty.

Before anyone else could speak out, Kane interjected. "I, for one, will be barring the clan wolves from leaving. If Sirius does not close the border, I will force the clan to stay in Misty Vale for their protection, if necessary. But I would prefer not to have to force them. So I would be grateful if Sirius would close the border."

Lily spoke out next, "I am glad that Sirius is willing to put himself in harm's way to protect the haven," she said, nodding emphatically.

No one else spoke out, so Sirius ended by confirming, "I will be closing the border at dawn. I advise anyone who wishes to leave to do so before then. There will not be another opportunity."

Abbey didn't see Sirius the next day. She wasn't due to work, but she needed the distraction, so she messaged both Lydia and Rick to see if anyone wanted her to cover a shift. Thankfully, Rick had messaged back that he would love to finish at lunchtime. Abbey had accepted at once and cycled her bike to the village.

"Are you okay?" Lydia asked her when she arrived.

"Yes," Abbey replied. She didn't think Sirius would appreciate her revealing even the most innocent details of his plan to anyone. "I just needed a distraction from thinking about the danger to Misty Vale," Abbey told her.

Abbey worked quietly for the rest of the day. Whenever her thoughts turned to Sirius and what he had told her the night before, she pushed them away. When Lydia turned the sign to closed, Abbey told her she would look after the clean-up and would lock up after her. Lydia was a good friend, but Abbey was aware that she had been taking advantage of the friendship while investigating Jimmy's death. She was happy to repay Lydia with this small favour.

Abbey arrived home after her short cycle. She had leftovers from the diner for her dinner. She made herself a cup of tea and finally let her thoughts drift back to last night.

She had not slept well; her brain had not been able to switch off. Everything Sirius had told her kept running through her mind. Sirius was over one thousand years old! She could not even comprehend such an age. What would he be like when the memories of all those years settled back inside him. He said he had been removed from humanity when he held the memories of three hundred years of life.

With a thousand years of life, how would anyone be able to relate to him? He had said even the oldest vampires were like children to him when he had been three hundred. He said he would be dangerous to everyone, including her.

Abbey wanted to not believe this, but she did. She had to admit to herself that part of her was afraid. What if, by drawing back his memories, Sirius became even more dangerous to Misty Vale than the wizard who was trying to break the sanctuary. And could Sirius become dangerous not only to Misty Vale but to the entire world? Was the cure worse than the disease?

Chapter 21

Abbey was waiting for Sirius at the Misty Vale beach when he arrived at dawn. She had been there for thirty minutes in fear that she would miss him. He stepped out of his car. "I did not expect to see you here," he said.

"I felt a need to be here. I don't know why." She shrugged. "I suppose it is something about being here at the beginning and at the end."

He gave her a self-deprecating smile. "Hopefully not the end Abbey," he said. "However, if you wish to join me while I work the incantation, you are welcome." He indicated for her to go first across the border to Ballybunion.

Abbey stood at the top of the cliff. She assumed that this was part of Sirius's magic, as she normally found herself at the beach beside the cliff, not on top of it. Sirius stood beside her. "You should not touch me while I am drawing and releasing the magic. You could be harmed by the hex as I invoke it."

Abbey nodded and stood back.

Sirius didn't reach the ground this time while he worked his magic. He stood there on the cliff, his hands drawn up towards the sky. Around his feet, vines began to form. A wind manifested from nowhere and blew around him but did not touch Abbey. A blue fire materialized from his right hand, shooting to the sky, and finally, a swirl of water appeared from his left hand.

He then began to speak in the same unfamiliar language Abbey had heard him use

157

previously. His voice was low as he spoke. The vines grew up his legs to his upward-facing hands and snaked around them. Then, the wind, which had been blowing all around, concentrated in his hands. He pushed them closer together, and all four elements combined between his two hands. A ball of liquid blue fire formed. On the surface of the ball, Abbey could see images of trees. His voice started to rise, and as it did, the ball grew larger.

With his voice at a crescendo, the ball became a stream of liquid blue. Sirius brought his hands down in front of him, and the blue liquid shot from his hands. He turned in a circle, the stream leaving his hands and forming a barrier along the beach below the cliff.

When it was done, Sirius fell to his knees, and Abbey moved to help. "Stay away, Abbey," he warned, his voice horse.

Abbey halted. She saw a shade of the vines creep down his body and back into the earth. Then, a slight breeze ruffled his hair and clothing before it dissipated. A spirit of a blue flame formed in his right hand before disappearing in a haze of smoke and water drizzled from his left hand, leaving only the smell of petrichor behind.

He then stood. "It is done," he said.

He pointed Abbey to a portal which had formed there at the cliff. Abbey had not seen it before. "After you," he said. Abbey stepped through, and they were back in Misty Vale.

The next day, the alert went off. Abbey was at work when she spotted Sirius striding towards the beach. Without even a nod to Lily, she had thrown her apron off and ran from the diner to follow him.

"Who are you?" Abbey heard Sirius ask a young male as she stepped out of Misty Vale.

"I have to get in," the male said. He started waving his hands, and Abbey saw light flowing from them, but it didn't seem to be doing anything.

"Is he the wizard who placed the compulsion on Sarah?" Abbey asked.

"No," Sirius answered, "he is too young and would not have the strength to place such a strong compulsion and erase her memory. He is another victim."

"I have to get in," the male said again.

"Why do you have to get in?" Sirius asked.

"I have to get in," the male repeated.

"Why is he just repeating himself?" Abbey asked.

"He is under a compulsion," Sirius said.

"So what happens if he gets inside?" Abbey asked.

"He won't be able to break through the barrier, and because he is under a compulsion, he will keep trying until he dies," Sirius told her. Abbey gasped, and Sirius shook his head. He fished his phone from his pocket. "Lily, can you please come to Ballybunion. The portal is open," Sirius told Lily. "We will wait until Lily arrives," he said to Abbey.

159

Abbey sighed in relief on seeing Lily step through the barrier. The wizard had continued to throw magic with no effect. Even Abbey could now see the compulsion which pushed him to continue to try to get through. She didn't know what Sirius had planned, but she hoped that Lily would have the answer.

"I'm here," Lily said. "Who is he?"

"A wizard named Matthew. I didn't recognise him at first, but I met him a few years ago," Sirius said. "He is under a compulsion to get into Misty Vale. I assume if he does get through, he will then try to get to the source and draw energy from it to try to bring down the barrier," he told them.

"So what do you want to do?" Lily asked.

"I am hoping you have a sleeping potion in that bag," Sirius asked, pointing to the bag that Lily had brought through with her.

"I have a sleeping potion, but I am not sure it will be strong enough to bring him down when he is in such a state," Lily said, pointing to the wizard, who still kept repeating the same phrase.

"If you have a basic elixir, I can feed my magic into it, and it will super strength it," Sirius told her.

Lily put her hand in her bag and brought out two potions, one green and one red. She looked at the two potions and handed him the green one. "I recommend this one. It is meant to induce dreams," Lily said, handing it to Sirius. He held it between his two hands and muttered some words. He handed it to Abbey.

She raised her eyebrows, looking down at the bottle.

"Lily, step back," Sirius said. "Abbey, I am going to release the barrier, and I will hold him with my magic. It will be up to you to get the potion down his throat," he said.

"What!" Abbey said, was he crazy! She was not a wizard. How was she meant to get him to drink the potion?

"You heard me," Sirius confirmed. "Are you ready?" he asked.

Abbey took a deep breath and nodded. What else could she do? She couldn't expect the older woman to do it. And Sirius would be busy using his magic to hold the younger wizard in place. She only hoped that she didn't spill it!

Sirius waved his hands, and like magic, the barrier disappeared! The wizard fell forward and landed at Sirius's feet. He jumped up immediately, and Sirius waved his hands again, and the wizard was held there. "Quick now, Abbey, I won't be able to hold him for long."

Abbey pulled the stopper from the bottle and stepped forward. The wizard began to struggle against Sirius's magic, squirming. Abbey reached up for his mouth; he was moving jerkily, and he tried to get away from her. She held his jaw as tight as she could and poured the liquid down his throat. She then reached out and held his nose, remembering her mother doing the same when she was a child.

The wizard swallowed, and Abbey stepped away. He struggled on for a few more moments and then dropped to the ground, fast asleep.

Sirius stopped his magic, and he reached for the younger wizard and threw him over his shoulder. He strode to the portal and stepped through. Lily went next, and with a sigh of relief, Abbey followed them.

"I have my car," Lily said. They all three walked to Lily's car, Sirius with the young wizard still over his shoulder.

"If you could bring us to my home," Sirius suggested. "I will watch over him until he wakes and ensure that the compulsion has left him. I think it best for him to stay in Misty Vale until this is over. I will set up a barrier on my home to keep him there until I feel it is safe to release him," Sirius said and put Matthew in the back seat of the car.

"I best get back to work," Abbey said, looking at the diner.

"Yes," Sirius agreed, "there is nothing else to be done at the moment. I will draw the magic tonight after the bar closes."

Abbey sat at a table in the bar alone. She had arrived just in time for last orders. She was waiting for Sirius to arrive. He arrived as the second to last customer left. Abbey being the last.

"So, do you draw your memories now?" she asked Sirius.

"Yes," he said, "but you cannot be here for this part."

Abbey saw Tobias enter the bar.

"I can't?" she asked.

"I have told you already, Abbey, I will be dangerous. Although Tobias is not as strong as I will be with my magic and memories restored, he is the next strongest being in Misty Vale. If I become uncontrolled, he may be able to halt me long enough for some part of my humanity to reassert itself," Sirius said.

Abbey sighed, but she knew that there was no other action she could take but to go away. She saw Bill and Sarah come from behind the bar.

"Are you staying?" Abbey asked them.

"No," Bill replied, "we are going to Tobias's house until it is over. The bar will be closed until it is safe," he said. Abbey noticed the bag over his back and the one on Sarah's arm.

"Oh," she said, "okay."

Tobias arrived beside them, his eyes wide and brow furrowed. "I did not expect to see you here?" he said, echoing Sirius's words on finding her there.

"I am leaving now," she said. She reached for Sirius's hands, holding both of them in hers. She said, "Be safe, Sirius." Without speaking further, she turned to Bill and Sarah and left with them.

Chapter 22

Abbey had not seen Sirius since he had restored his memories. The alert must have gone off again, she thought as she saw him striding towards the barrier to Ballybunion. He did not look like the same man. He was not like a man at all. He was walking, but it was more like Misty Vale was moving out of his way. He was the magic; he was not human. This was what he knew he would become when his magic and memories were restored. It was terrifying, and everything in Abbey wanted to run. But no, not everything, because some tiny part of her wanted to follow him. Maybe that minuscule part of her that knew Sirius was still in there. He stepped through the barrier and fighting herself, she went through as well.

Sirius was standing on the beach; the tide was starting to turn, and the water was flowing inwards, drowning the sand. A group of five teenage boys were throwing themselves at the barrier. Even from where she stood behind Sirius, she could see that they were out of their minds. Abbey thought for a moment that it must be drugs, but how would they even know about the barrier.

She recalled how Belinda had told her Kate had described Sarah that day. Blank. They looked blank. They were under a compulsion from the wizard. He must have known about the alert and was looking for weaknesses without showing himself. He was using these teenagers.

Abbey heard Sirius begin to mutter. She looked at him, and his face was a mask of indifference. Abbey knew from his face that he intended to destroy them. They were nothing to him. "Sirius, no," she cried, placing herself in front of the boys.

He looked down at her. "I will kill them," he told her, his voice devoid of any emotion.

"No, Sirius, you can't," Abbey cried.

"Who are you, little human," he sneered at her, "to halt me? You are as unimportant as these beings." He laughed. "But perhaps you can be amusing," he intoned. He grabbed her and pulled her towards him, pushing his mouth to hers in a bruising parody of a kiss.

Abbey struggled to get away from him, but he held her against him. She was not strong enough to hold him off. He was not her Sirius. He was something else. She should have stayed away. With a sense of relief, she felt him pulling back from her. It was not that he had pulled back but that Tobias had arrived and he had dragged Sirius away from her.

"Go," Tobias told her, and she ran back through to Misty Vale.

Abbey pulled the keys to the diner from her pocket, her hands shaking. It took three tries to unlock the door, but she finally got inside. She leaned against the door, catching her breath. She stayed there for a few minutes. Her breath catching in her throat, but she would not let herself cry. Sirius had told her that he would not be himself. She prayed that when this was over, he would be able to find his way back.

Moving away from the door, Abbey made herself a cup of tea and sat down at a table. She let her head drop to the table.

The diner bell rang, and Abbey looked up, her heart beating rapidly. Abbey placed a hand to her heart, relieved to see it was Tobias.

"Did you manage to stop him?" she asked, feeling guilty for leaving the boys there but knowing there was nothing she could have done.

"Yes," he said. "It was very dangerous to have followed him," Tobias scolded.

"I know," Abbey said, "but if I hadn't, those boys would be dead."

Tobias sighed deeply. "Probably," he said.

"Did you know it would be that bad?" Abbey asked.

"Yes and no," Tobias told her. "I am nearly three hundred years old. I have been in Misty Vale for over two hundred years. Sirius described me to you as the oldest resident of Misty Vale. But I believe you now know that Sirius himself is the oldest resident. But I have been here continuously for all that time. I remember meeting vampires who were the age I am now before I arrived in Misty Vale, and they were dark. Dark and cold and inhuman.

"I met Sirius when he was nearly eight hundred. I told him that I had come here because I did not want to turn into those vampires. Not long afterwards, he confided in me his age and his connection with this place. He also told me that the haven itself would help me in some way to keep my humanity. He promised me that he would use his magic to help if I ever needed it."

Abbey listened in silence, nodding occasionally to show her understanding.

"Fifty years ago, I asked Sirius to come back to Misty Vale. I told him I was struggling," Tobias said, looking her directly in the eyes. "I was losing touch, I was afraid," he told her. "Sirius came," he said, raising one of his hands to his forehead, "and he removed some of my memories." He smiled at her, and a light that had been missing from his eyes returned. "I felt an ease," he laid a hand on his heart, "and I started to live again." He sighed again.

"So yes, some part of me knew how bad it would be because of my own experience with darkness. But I was not yet three hundred. Sirius is much older. And therefore, no, I didn't know how bad it would be. I have never experienced a wizard who was more than three hundred years old. But I will tell you this: Sirius is the best friend I have ever had, and I believe that I am his closest friend. He has a trust with Lily, and she knows he is a protector of Misty Vale, but she docs not know he is the founder. It is clear that he has now placed the same trust in you that he once placed in me by revealing his secret. I do not believe there is anyone else in the entire world who knows who Sirius is. And I am telling you now that I will find a way to bring him back," he said, reaching out and taking both her hands in his. "I believe that you will be key to that," he said.

"I will do anything," Abbey told him. He nodded, got up, and left.

Abbey took a sip of her tea, but it had gone cold.

Abbey sat in her garden, breathing in the fresh air, when Tobias appeared. She had gone home not long after their conversation the day before and had not left since. She had told herself she had jobs to do around the house, but deep down, she knew she was hiding from Sirius.

"Hello, Abbey," Tobias said. "I hope you are well?" he asked.

She smiled and tapped on the seat beside her for him to join her, and he sat down. "I am fine," she said. "How is Sirius?" she asked.

"He is at home," he told her. "He intends to stay there working on his magic until such time as the wizard has been dealt with."

"Is the young wizard, Matthew, still with him?" she asked.

"Yes," Tobias confirmed, "and he is awake. I think having someone else there is a good thing. It seems to be helping Sirius."

She took a deep breath and let it out. "That's good," she said.

"He has not said anything, but I believe that our Sirius is still in there," he told her. "I think he is aware that after this is finished, he will not want to have done anything he cannot take back. I imagine he is staying away from everyone to protect all of the residents of Misty Vale."

168

"He is in there?" she asked quietly.

"Yes, I think so." he patted her hand and stood up. "I wanted to come and check on you," he said. "I am glad to see you are well," he told her, and with a nod, he bid her farewell.

Chapter 23

The next two days were quiet. She had not seen Sirius since the incident on the beach. For which she was grateful. After what Tobias had told her, Abbey believed Sirius staying at home was only a positive thing for all of Misty Vale. The longer that nothing happened, the more the tension rose in Abbey. She was jittery and couldn't focus on any one thing. She worked in the diner for the two days, but she was surprised Lydia hadn't docked her wages because she got so many orders wrong.

It was at dawn the next morning that she felt it. Like an earthquake, the land of Misty Vale shuddered. Abbey knew what it was. Sirius was pulling power, more power than he had ever drawn from Misty Vale before. The dark wizard, as she had named him in her head, had arrived, and Sirius was preparing to do battle. She jumped from her bed and threw on her clothes. She didn't bother to wash or brush her hair. There was no time for that. She needed to be there. Not at the battle, but here at Misty Vale, waiting for Sirius to return.

Abbey stood across from the beach at Misty Vale and watched as Sirius arrived. He didn't even glance her way. Abbey felt a stab in her heart, but he had told her she was unimportant. She was nothing to him. Part of her still wanted to follow him, but this time, she hesitated. She just stood and watched.

"He will need you at the end," Tobias said from behind her. "You need to go through," he said, his blue eyes filled with sorrow. "I will protect you," he promised her.

Abbey nodded, and Tobias stepped forward and offered her his hand. Abbey took it, and they stepped together into Ballybunion.

Sirius stood stock still on the cliff. Facing him was a male, his light blond hair blowing around his face. At first, Abbey thought it was being blown by the wind, but then she noticed there was no wind. It was the dark wizard's magic that was blowing his hair. Sirius's hair was still, but Abbey could feel the magic radiating from him. Unlike when he had performed the ritual to protect the barrier, there were no outward signs of his power.

"Maddox," Sirius said, his tone indolent, "I did not expect to see you at Misty Vale again," he said.

Abbey could not see his face nor the face of the other wizard, but she saw the male shrug his shoulders. "I thought it might be time for another visit," he said. His English had a slight accent, which Abbey thought might be French.

"I believe I told you the last time that you would never be welcomed here?" Sirius said. This time, Abbey heard an edge to his words.

"You remember last time?" Maddox asked. "I had heard you had offloaded your memories. I must have been misinformed." Maddox had only finished his last word when he put his hands up in front of his body and started to mutter. Abbey was too far away to hear what he was saying or even what language he was speaking. She braced herself for Sirius to be hit with fire or thunder. But instead of an attack being pushed at Sirius, Maddox instead pulled something from him.

Sirius stumbled; whatever Maddox was doing, Sirius had not been prepared for it. Abbey gasped. She knew then what was happening. The dark wizard was pulling Sirius's magic from him. Sirius's power was draining from him to Maddox. Abbey felt real fear: would Sirius die here without even a retaliatory attack. But then Sirius seemed to shake it off, his whole body filled with light, and he pushed the light from himself to Maddox. The dark wizard started to shake, and Abbey thought maybe Sirius had defeated him. But these had only been the openers, then the battle began in earnest.

In truth, Abbey couldn't see or comprehend most of what was happening. The air vibrated around them, and they were caught in a kaleidoscope of colours. A rumbling groan from the earth filled her ears. And all around them, a phantasmagoria of images appeared: wild animals and carnivorous plants and thorn bushes. Fires red, blue, and white manifested, and Abbey stepped further away, feeling the heat even from where she stood.

No words mumbled or shouted were spoken by either wizard now. Abbey understood that this was a different level of magic. This was the magic at its most elemental. They were drawing on the pure force of magic, and it was terrifying to behold. Abbey wanted to run, but she could not pull her eyes from the battle waging in front of her. She didn't know how long it had continued. She felt her legs shaking but was unsure if it was from fear or because she had stood unmoving for so long.

And then it halted. The images disappeared, the land grew still, and silence filled the air. And the wizard lay at Sirius's feet. Abbey thought for a moment he was dead, but then she heard his ragged breath.

"You have learnt much since we last fought," Sirius said, his tone the same as the indolence he had used before. "But not enough, I think." He raised his hands, and Abbey knew this would be the killing shot. But before he could deal his final blow, the dark wizard disappeared. Sirius collapsed.

Abbey went to run to him, but Tobias, with his vampire speed, got there first. Abbey knew then that Sirius's final words had been a bluff. He was gravely depleted.

Tobias picked him up, and Abbey could see the land on the top of the cliff was scorched. The portal was still open, and they stepped through, bringing Sirius back to Misty Vale.

"Bring me to the source," Sirius said.

Abbey was relieved to see Bill come running out of the bar. She didn't think that Tobias was strong enough to carry Sirius's dead weight all the way. Tobias passed Sirius off to Bill, stretching his shoulders and giving Abbey a

173

little smile. "Bring him to the source," Abbey said.

Bill nodded, moving to the bar faster than Abbey, even though he was carrying Sirius. But everyone knew that werewolves were really strong. Vampires, not so much, she thought.

He went straight to the kitchen, and Sirius grunted, directing him to the location of the source. Sirius told him to lay him on the spot. There was no sign of anything different at that site, unlike the last time when Abbey had followed Sirius there and seen him performing magic over it.

This time, Sirius did not perform any magic with his hands. Instead, light filled the whole area around him. It looked like one light was flowing from his head into the source, and a different light was flowing from the source to his body. It seemed to take a long time, and Abbey felt the ground shaking beneath her feet as the magic flowed. And then it stopped, the light and source disappearing.

Sirius lay there for a moment longer, then getting to his feet, still looking pale, he said, "I will be okay now."

Bill nodded and walked out of the kitchen. Tobias patted Sirius on the shoulder. "You had me worried for a minute there, old man," he said. He gave Abbey a quick hug and left, too. Abbey suddenly felt awkward. Should she go? She thought, but Sirius saw her hesitation and said, "Please stay, Abbey. I will see you home."

They walked together from the kitchen into the bar. Sarah stood there beside Bill. "Sarah," Sirius said, "you are now the protector of the source." The young woman trembled but nodded. "I will be here to support you for as long as you need," Sirius told her.

"Thank you," Sarah said, pushing her shoulders back and looking Sirius directly in the eyes.

Abbey knew that Sarah would rise to the challenge of protector. Misty Vale's magic had selected her because she had it in her.

"Shall we go?" Sirius asked Abbey. She nodded, and he offered her his arm. Even though he had been the one who had been hurt, Abbey's legs were still shaking from the fear and adrenaline of the morning, and she took his arm gratefully.

They went outside, and Sirius's car was waiting. Abbey wondered if he had called it there by magic. "Oh good," he said. "Tobias has dropped my car for me." Abbey smothered a laugh when she had imagined that Sirius had a magically self-driving car!

They arrived at Abbey's house, and Sirius got out as well and walked Abbey to her door. He stopped there, and Abbey looked at him.

"There is one thing I must put right," he said softly. And he bent down and placed a gentle kiss on her lips. Abbey moaned, and he drew her closer, and the kiss deepened, and then it ended, and he stepped back.

"Abbey, I will visit you as soon as I can," Sirius told her. "I will need some time to recover," he said.

Abbey nodded. After that kiss, she didn't know what to say. Stepping in her door, she saw her notebook on the table. She opened it and saw the three questions she had written that first day.

Why dump the body? She now knew this had been part of Maddox's plan to disrupt the haven of Misty Vale.

Who would want to kill Jimmy? The wizard to remove the protector of the source.

What did Jimmy know or do to get him killed? The answer was simple: protect Misty Vale.

Chapter 24

Abbey woke the next morning to knocking at her door. This was becoming a habit, Abbey thought. But she hoped like hell it wasn't another person trying to confess to killing Jimmy! She spent another sleepless night. She had thought now that the dark wizard had been defeated, she would be able to sleep. But her brain kept her awake thinking about Sirius and the kiss.

Abbey opened the door, and Sirius was standing there. He looked better, back to himself. He gave Abbey a slight smile. "Hello, Abbey," he said.

"Hello, Sirius," she replied and stepped back, letting him inside.

"I shouldn't have called so early," he said. "Why don't I make some coffee," he suggested, "while you get ready for the day? Don't rush," he said.

Abbey agreed, but she did rush. She had a splash-and-dash shower and pulled on jeans and a sweater. She pulled a brush through her hair and went to join him. He had the coffee ready.

"I was sure that you would want to know who the wizard was," he said. "I half expected you to be at my door at dawn."

"I would have been if I had thought you would be recovered enough to talk to me," Abbey agreed, pouring herself a cup of coffee and helping herself to milk and sugar.

"The wizard is Maddox," Sirius said, not waiting for Abbey to take a sip of her coffee.

177

Abbey nodded to indicate she was listening. She had heard Sirius calling him Maddox on the cliff.

"He tried to gain access to Misty Vale two hundred years ago," he stated. "Misty Vale barred him from entry, and he appealed to me to speak to whoever was in charge on his behalf. He did not understand that the magic of Misty Vale is not under anyone's control. I could if I used my magic to overrule it, but I would not," he told her. "I knew that he was not looking for a haven, that instead, he sought to take the magic of the source for himself. So I told him that not only would I not intervene, but I would turn all of my magic against him rather than allow him entry." Sirius sighed. "I did not need to draw my magic from Misty Vale to stop him at that time. He was much younger than he is now." He paused, looking at Abbey to be sure she was following.

Abbey simply nodded again without speaking.

"He has grown stronger, and his ambition is unchanged. He wants the source," he told her.

"But you defeated him," Abbey said.

"Yes," Sirius agreed. "For now, but I didn't kill him. He did not realize how close he came. I have grown complacent. He will be back," Sirius told her.

Abbey's shoulders slumped; she had hoped that was the end of it.

"I don't know when he will be back," he said. "It might not be within your lifetime."

Abbey's head pulled back. She had not thought of that. Her lifetime and Sirius's lifetime were very different things. Sirius was over a thousand years old. She was thirty-five, but one day, she would be seventy, and he would not have aged from how he was now. Abbey placed her hand on her chest, trying to hold back a pain she did not want to acknowledge.

Sirius continued, "It might be next year." Sirius shook his head. "Abbey, having my memories back was painful," he told her. "What made me inhuman was not only the power but the loss. In my long life, I have loved and lost many times. When all of that loss is held in one heart, it turns hard and closed and fearful. You know that you will never let yourself feel such suffering again. That, more than anything, is the curse of a life such as mine. Those memories are gone now, but the pain of them is still with me. I don't know when that pain will fade away," he said, shaking his head.

"Abbey, you need to know that I can never love. And not only because of the fear of loss but there is also Misty Vale. My magic sustains it. What many wizards do not know is that love, true love, is the reason wizards start to lose their magic and die. If I ever truly love, I will start to age, and I will die, and Misty Vale will die with me.

And with those words, Abbey knew that she had fallen for Sirius.

Continue reading now for sneak peak of the Misty Vale Mysteries Book 2

Chapter 1

Abbey handed Kathy her coffee.

"There's a body on the beach."

Abbey looked up at hearing these words from her boss, Lydia. Who had only now arrived for her shift. Abbey pulled off her apron and ran to the diner door. Her thoughts jumping to Sarah. Had the magical protection placed on her by Sirius and Lily failed?

Abbey's breath escaped her in a gasp. She placed a hand to her chest to calm her rapidly beating heart. It was the body of a male, and not Sarah who lay there. Abbey could see his dark hair and muscular body. But she could not tell who it was. Two males and one female were standing beside the body. Abbey recognised Carter as one of the males. But she did not recognise the other. The female was a witch who sometimes came to the diner, but Abbey didn't know her name.

Abbey approached slowly, "who found him?" she asked. Carter looked up at Abbey's words. He shuffled away from the body and over to her. She had only met Carter for the first time a few weeks ago. He had told her at the time about seeing Jimmy the night before he had been murdered. But he had been a frequent customer at the diner since then. He was a quiet, gentle, male.

She still didn't know what type of supernatural he was, but with his slight physique, he was certainly not a werewolf.

"It's Sam Waters," Carter told her. "He lives across from me," he said, his voice shaking, as he forced the words past his lips. He was as pale as a ghost and looked like he might faint.

Abbey recognised the name. When she had re-entered Misty Vale that first time, beginning to accept that Misty Vale was an enchanted place, Sam had come over and introduced himself. He had explained that five years previously, he had been in her position. A normal human who had found himself in Misty Vale. It had been Sam who had convinced her what the others were. Vampires, witches, wizards, and werewolves.

Abbey's eyes filled with tears, he had been kind to her and had helped her to adjust in those first few weeks in Misty Vale. Abbey could not think who would want to kill him. He was only a human.

"Has anyone told Sirius?" she asked, pushing back her tears. She looked at Lydia, who shook her head.

"I don't have his number," Carter told her.

Abbey wasn't sure what to do. Should she ask everyone to step away from Sam's body, to preserve the scene for Lily, or go back to the diner to get her phone to ring Lily and Sirius?

"I'll get your phone," Lydia offered.

Abbey nodded thanks to Lydia and walked over to the male and female who still stood beside

181

Sam. Abbey introduced herself and saw recognition enter their eyes. She had gained some notoriety in Misty Vale due to her involvement with Jimmy's murder. She had found his body and had investigated his murder with the help of Sirius and Lily. Lily as a witch and a doctor had been able to carry out an autopsy on Jimmy's body.

"I think it best that we all stay as far away as possible from the body," Abbey advised. "We don't want to contaminate the scene and results of the medical examination."

At these words they both scurried away from Sam. Abbey walked over to meet Lydia, glad to see her arrive with the phone. She dialled Sirius's number. He picked up after two rings.

"Abbey," he said, sounding winded.

"There's a body on the Misty Vale beach," Abbey replied, without any greeting.

"Have you rung Lily?" he asked, his voice deadpan.

"She's the next call," Abbey confirmed.

"I am on my way," he said and hung up without a goodbye.

Abbey dialled Lily and told her about the body and Lily agreed to come at once.

Abbey looked around wishing Sirius would hurry as she shooed another male away from Sam's body. What was wrong with people wanting to look at this? He was the fourth person; she'd had to move along. Abbey's shoulders relaxed; spotting Sirius's car pull up at the beach. She had kept her eyes averted from Sam's body. She did not want to remember him that way.

182

Abbey had already heard the speculations being shared by the onlookers, but she refused to listen.

Sirius strode onto the beach, raising his hands, his lips moving silently. Light flowed from his hands and encased Sam's body and the area around him. The spectators whom Abbey hadn't been able to move on completely, stepped back further. Sirius's magic was impressive, even to the supernatural denizens of Misty Vale. Abbey sighed in relief; the scene was safe for Lily to examine.

"Hello Abbey," Sirius said, his voice devoid of emotion.

"Hello Sirius," Abbey replied. It had been six weeks since she had last seen him. He had visited her after Maddox, or the dark wizard, as Abbey thought of him, had been defeated. He had told her at the time that no relationship was possible between them. Seeing him now, Abbey put a hand up to her heart, soothing the stab of pain. Sirius's cold greeting could only be seen as confirmation that nothing had changed. No something had changed; he had never before looked at her with cold eyes. Abbey had understood what he had told her. She could only respect his devotion to Misty Vale. But some part of her wanted him to be sad about not being with her. Was that wrong of her? Now it seemed he had gotten over it. Abbey mentally shook herself. Sam had been murdered, and here she was mooning over Sirius like a teenager.

"Did you find the body?" Sirius asked, and Abbey thought for a second she had detected a note of concern.

"No, it was Carter," Abbey replied, nodding her head to where Carter sat on the sand as far away from Sam as he could. Abbey spied Lily's little car sputtering to a stop beside them.

"Who is it?" Lily asked, as she jogged towards them.

"Sam Waters," Abbey replied.

Lily sighed and shook her head. "Release your magic Sirius and let me at the body," Lily told him. Sirius waved his hands and the light encasing the body dissipated. Lily gave Abbey a nod and without another word went to perform the examination.

"Why don't you take Carter to the diner," Sirius suggested. "I will clear away the gawkers."

Abbey nodded her agreement, happy to escape the scene, she joined Carter. He still looked pale, and he was shaking. Abbey thought he might be in shock. "Why don't you come with me to the diner?" she suggested, and Carter nodded. Abbey thought that she should offer him an arm in case he fainted. But thought he might be offended by the offer. So, she walked beside him instead. Lydia had returned to the diner once she had given Abbey her phone, and seeing them approaching, she held the door open for them.

"Sit down both of you," Lydia said. Abbey sat down with Carter at a table at the back of the diner. For once the smell of the food cooking did not bring her comfort. She sank gratefully into the

184

soft cushion of the chair. She didn't ask him any questions for the moment. She could see that Lydia was making Carter some of the tea he liked. Abbey thought it was best to let him have some before she started questioning him.

Lydia arrived with the tea, while she was serving it, Abbey sent Lily a message, asking her to come and check on Carter. □

"How are you feeling now?" Abbey asked, once Carter had finished his tea. The colour had returned to his face and Abbey assumed by this that Carter was not a vampire. He was definitely not a werewolf with his slim figure, so he must be a witch or wizard.

"A bit better," Carter confirmed.

"You found Sam?" Abbey prompted.

Carter put a hand up to cover his eyes and then lowered it to cover his mouth. He nodded, dropping his hand from his face. "I was running on the beach," he said, looking Abbey directly in the eyes. "I like to start the day with a run, before I pick up tea at the diner," he said. "I saw him from a distance, but I didn't realise he was dead. I thought," he stuttered, "I thought he was only resting on the beach, until I was nearly upon him," he halted for a moment. "There was nothing I could do," he implored, his eyes downcast, "he was already gone," he said, raising a finger to the middle of his forehead in an unusual gesture.

Abbey nodded, "I understand," she said, reaching over and touching his hand. Now that she was sure he was not a vampire, she thought it was okay to touch him. "How did you know he was gone?"

Carter raised a hand to his head and tapped a finger at a point in the middle of his forehead again. "I knew he was gone," Carter said. Abbey thought she was meant to understand something from this. But before she could question him

186

further, the door to the diner opened to admit Lily and Sirius.

They didn't come directly over but went towards the bathrooms instead. Abbey assumed they wanted to wash their hands after dealing with Sam's body. Sirius had move Sam's body to his car, and cover him with a blanket, before they entered the diner. Sirius exited the bathrooms first, but he held back from approaching them. Lily came out and walked straight over to Abbey and Carter.

Lily sat down beside them, "now how are you young man?" she asked.

"I'm feeling better," Carter replied.

Lily reached over and took his wrist in her hand and looking at her watch she started counting under her breath. "Your pulse is okay. It was only the shock, I think, and you are getting over that now?" Lily asked.

"Yes," he replied.

Lily nodded to Sirius, and he joined them at the table.

"Do you feel well enough to tell us how you found him?" Sirius asked.

Carter nodded and repeated what he had told Abbey about being out for a run and coming across Sam's body. "I knew he was gone," he said, and Sirius and Lily both nodded.

"What am I missing," Abbey asked. "How could you know he was gone?"

All three turned their faces to Abbey and they all held quizzical looks. Carter's frown cleared first and understanding dawned in his expression.

"I'm an empath," he said, "I thought you knew that? I told you about Jimmy seeming worried, the night before he was murdered," he said.

"Oh," Abbey replied, "no, I didn't know that was what you meant. What type?" Abbey started to ask but decided this was not the right time. "Lily, can you tell us how Sam died?" she asked instead.

Lily looked around the diner, there were no other customers close to them. But some of the residents of Misty Vale had better than human hearing. Sirius waved his hands around and the air around Abbey started to vibrate. Sirius seemed to be using his magic much more than he had, previous to the fight with the dark wizard.

"He has been drained of all his blood," Lily replied.

Carter's face bleached of all colour again. Abbey brought a hand up to cover her mouth, holding in a gasp of shock. Abbey looked at Sirius, his face showed no emotion on hearing this news. Abbey wondered if he was untouched by the horror or if Lily had already told him?

"Was he murdered in Ballybunion?" Abbey asked.

Lily shook her head, "no, he was murdered here, on the beach. No attempt was made to hide the evidence," Lily told them.□

Buy now on Amazon continue reading
https://a.co/d/hkWwP1q

Misty Vale, where supernatural creatures coexist with humans, a chilling mystery unfolds in Misty Vale Mysteries Book 2: "Misty Vale's Bloody Secret."

When a lifeless body, completely drained of blood, is discovered on the beach of Misty Vale, a wave of unease crashes over the community. Suspicion and fear grip the hearts of both humans and vampires alike.

Abbey finds herself at the centre of the investigation. When a second victim, another normal human, is discovered drained of life. Abbey wonders if she will become the next unfortunate casualty in this sinister game.

Determined to protect herself and those she holds dear, Abbey embarks on a quest for truth, delving into the hidden corners of Misty Vale's supernatural underbelly. With the clock ticking and the stakes rising, Abbey must navigate a treacherous landscape of ancient rivalries and deceptive alliances to unmask the malevolent force behind the bloody secret.

Join Abbey as she unravels the enigma shrouding Misty Vale, unveiling secrets that threaten to tear the town apart and jeopardize her own existence. Will she uncover the truth in time, or will Misty Vale succumb to its darkest secrets?

The magical county of Kerry in the west of Ireland was my inspiration for this series of books. I spent many of my childhood summers in the town of Listowel were my great aunt had been the district nurse. The family always visited Ballybunion during our time in Kerry. In my memories it never rained, even as I recall my mother saying "if it rains again next year. We won't come the year after." Thankfully, the year after never came and the family returned again and again to the beautiful beach of Ballybunion. If you enjoyed this book or any of the books in this series, I would be grateful if you would leave a review.

I hope you will join me again in the magical adventures of Misty Vale.

Review Your Purchases (amazon.com)

For updates on release date and bonus material giving updates from all your favourite Misty Vales residents, join my mailing list:
http://subscribepage.io/nkfiBj

For more updates from follow me on Facebook:
https://www.facebook.com/profile.php?id=100093678642092

Follow me on Amazon to keep up to date with Misty Vale Mysteries Book 3 release date.

Printed in Great Britain
by Amazon

32472389R00106